MARQV NEVES

The Jacksons' Debate

Contents

Foreword by Dr. Sabine Brels, Founding Director of World Animal Justice

"A truly innovative fiction that deeply challenges the treatment of other animal species"

The Jacksons' Debate by Marqv Neves is a thought-provoking novella that pushes the boundaries of speculative fiction to explore ethics, environmentalism, and the complexities of human-animal relationships. Through its unconventional narrative, the book invites readers to examine humanity from the perspective of an alien race, the Jacksons, whose sophisticated moral and philosophical inquiries expose the uncomfortable parallels between their debates and our own treatment of other animal species.

The story introduces the Jacksons as meticulous and ethically conscious beings grappling with humanity's potential as a dietary resource while simultaneously engaging with orcas to understand interspecies ethics. Characters like Marvin Jackson, a nutritionist, and Grag and Gunnar, philosophers and ethicists, explore humanity's physiology and societal constructs. Their experiments on human subjects, including Taylor Swift and Arthur Neves, are handled with care but lead to unforeseen ethical dilemmas, such as societal upheaval caused by their absences. These scenarios highlight the unpredictable complexity of human behavior, sparking a debate among the Jacksons about the morality of their actions.

Simultaneously, the Jacksons' interactions with orcas, led by Glugi Jackson, use advanced telepathic technology to uncover the orcas' perspectives on human environmental impact. These interviews reveal profound insights into humanity's destructive tendencies, such as pollution and exploitative behaviors, juxtaposed with the orcas' harmonious and environmentally respectful culture. This contrast deepens the ethical quandary facing the Jacksons: Can humans be treated as a resource when they demonstrate such complex emotional and societal structures?

Perspectives for Animal Rights Advocacy

The novella offers a powerful framework for advocating animal rights by challenging the reader to confront their own anthropocentric biases. By reversing the roles—placing humans under the ethical scrutiny of a more advanced species—it reveals the ethical inconsistencies in our treatment of other sentient beings. The Jacksons' rigorous debates about whether humans can ethically be consumed echo the questions animal rights advocates pose about the morality of factory farming, animal experimentation, and habitat destruction.

The ethical lens of *The Jacksons' Debate* can inspire animal advocates to:

1. **Promote Empathy Through Perspective Shifts**: The Jacksons' confusion over human practices such as clothing and shame invites readers to reflect on how human judgments of other species' behaviors are often rooted in ignorance. This perspective fosters empathy and encourages a deeper understanding of non-human animals' needs and behaviors.

2. **Question Cultural Norms**: The novella critiques humanity's exploitation of the environment and other species through an alien lens, demonstrating how normalized practices, such as consuming animals or destroying ecosystems, can seem grotesque when viewed objectively. Advocates can use this approach to challenge societal norms and promote alternative, ethical ways of living.

3. **Address the Complexity of Sentience**: The Jacksons' discovery of human emotional and societal complexity parallels ongoing efforts to recognize the sentience of animals. The book supports the argument that animals are not commodities but individuals with intrinsic value, deserving of rights and protection.

Challenging Animal Treatment Worldwide

The Jacksons' Debate provides critical perspectives and tools to support animal rights advocacy:

- **Ethical Frameworks**: The Jacksons' meticulous ethical discussions can inspire frameworks for assessing the morality of animal-related policies and practices, ensuring that decisions are grounded in respect for sentience and autonomy.
- **Public Engagement**: The story's speculative fiction ap-

proach makes it accessible and engaging, allowing advocates to reach a broader audience by encouraging readers to question the status quo through creative storytelling.

- **Intersectional Advocacy**: By exploring parallels between human exploitation and animal suffering, the novella bridges the gap between environmental, social justice, and animal rights movements, reinforcing the interconnectedness of these issues.

A Call to Reflect and Act

The author masterfully uses speculative fiction to critique anthropocentrism and challenge readers' assumptions about ethical consumption. The Jacksons' debates mirror real-world discussions about animal rights, sustainable living, and the moral responsibilities of advanced societies. Their confusion over human behaviors underscores how alien our practices can appear when viewed through an objective lens, prompting readers to reflect on their own biases.

Ultimately, *The Jacksons' Debate* succeeds as both a literary and philosophical work. For animal rights advocates and movements, it is not just a story—it is a tool for reflection and action. It challenges us to reconsider our treatment of other animal species, offering a blueprint for advancing ethical practices that prioritize the well-being of all sentient beings. By using fiction as a catalyst for ethical self-reflection, Neves empowers readers to envision a world where justice extends beyond humanity to all life forms.

Prologue

Have you ever felt utterly, irrevocably insignificant? Like a particularly dull pebble on a beach teeming with infinitely more fascinating pebbles? We're not talking ironic pebbles here, or pebbles pondering their place in some grand cosmic design—those are far too busy being profound. No, we're talking about those regular, unremarkable pebbles completely oblivious to their own inherent pebbleness.

That feeling, that quiet, unsettling sense of being thoroughly, utterly ordinary—that's a starting point for what we're about to delve into. Brace yourself. This isn't your standard tale of valiant humans facing the cosmos armed with laser pistols and wry witticisms. This...is something far stranger, far more introspective.

The question isn't "What's out there?"

But rather: "What happens when what's out there...is deciding what to do with what's in here?"

Yes, you. Reading this. You're the "in here" part of the equation. And if you're expecting the kind of intergalactic encounter where the aliens show up and conveniently think, act, and break down complex moral dilemmas in a way easily digestible to the human palate... well, that's simply not on the menu.

This book doesn't offer those comforts.

Because the central uncomfortable truth is this: When it comes to interspecies relations — and by "interspecies" we really mean "everything that isn't human" — the monkeys don't get a say. The fish don't get a say. The pandas, the squirrels, the earthworms — they all exist in a world meticulously shaped and reshaped by human decisions, yet they have no voice in the matter. Their fates are sealed by the whims, values, and sometimes the sheer capriciousness of human discretion.

Humans, with their remarkable ability to narrativize, create hierarchies of worthiness among non-human beings. Consider the pandas, with their adorable, black-and-white countenances. These creatures are often the poster children of conservation efforts, their cuteness a currency that buys them a stay of execution in a world where many species are not so fortunate. Yet, have you ever pondered how odd it might seem to the pandas themselves, if they were aware of the reasons behind their protected status? Would they find it curious, perhaps even unsettling, that their survival hinges on human perceptions of their aesthetic appeal?

Now, contrast this with the plight of the fish. For centuries, humans have debated the sentience of fish, oscillating between seeing them as cold, unfeeling creatures and recognizing the subtle complexities of their behaviors. The fish, silently swimming through their watery realms, are entirely at the mercy of these debates, their worth and the moral considerations extended to them dictated solely by human discourse.

This is the crux of the matter: the inherent imbalance in who gets to have a say. Humans construct narratives around their own understanding, telling themselves comforting stories where they're the protagonists, the heroes, even when the evidence suggests they're more akin to that one guy at the galactic house party who spills the cosmic dip on the sentient rug and then tries to play it cool.

And now, consider if the roles were reversed. Imagine if another species, far more advanced, looked upon humanity with the same scrutinizing gaze. Imagine if they were the ones deciding whether humans were worthy of moral consideration, whether our quirks and complexities rendered us deserving of preservation or mere curiosities to be studied, commodified, or even consumed.

This story yanks the rug right out from under you.

The narrative you're about to engage with (or more accurately, be engaged by—remember, your vote's not exactly counting here)—takes as its starting point a radical shift in perspective. Or more precisely, the lack of it. You'll find no reassuring inner monologues from the "other." No attempts to soften the edges of a stark truth: sometimes beings, regardless of how evolved or morally enlightened they believe themselves to be, don't grant much thought at all to the "lesser" creatures under their metaphorical microscopes.

The reader's role here is an unsettling one. You become acutely aware of your own inherent human-ness, yearning for a voice, a platform to explain, justify, narrativize. But this story denies you that comfort. You're left to wrestle with the profound discomfort of not knowing "why."

The lack of readily available answers forces an unsettling kind of introspection. You become, in a sense, that pebble on the beach — observed, considered, acted upon — but never truly understood. And within that silence, a disturbing thought might just take root:

What if that's the point of the story all along?

The Ethical Dilemma of Human Meatballs

The grand hall of the Jacksons' Academy hummed with a low, pervasive frequency. It wasn't a sound that human ears could detect, but to the Jacksons, interconnected as they were through their intricate telepathic network, it was as palpable as the gentle pressure of their methane-rich atmosphere. Each thought, each observation, each subtle nuance of emotion, rippled across their collective consciousness, creating a symphony of data streams and analytical murmurs that filled the vast chamber.

At the center of the hall, a series of holographic displays flickered to life, bathing the assembled Jacksons in a cool, blue light. Graphs, charts, and anatomical diagrams shimmered in the air, their intricate details scrutinized by hundreds of multifaceted eyes. The air itself seemed to crackle with a subtle electrostatic charge, a testament to the intense mental energy that permeated the room.

The year was 2031. The Jacksons, masters of logic and efficiency, architects of a society that prided itself on harmony and
sustainability, found themselves facing a dilemma that defied
easy categorization. It wasn't a planetary crisis, a technological
malfunction, or even a particularly perplexing mathematical
theorem. It was a question of...diet.

The source of this dietary quandary? Humans.

The very notion of consuming these strange, seemingly illogical
creatures from a nearby planet had sparked a wave of debate that
rippled through Jacksonsonville's telepathic network, unsettling the usually calm waters of their collective consciousness.

The origin of this unsettling culinary proposition could be
traced back to the meticulously organized lab of Marvin Jackson, Jacksonsonville's most esteemed nutritionist. Marvin, a
Jackson known for his relentless pursuit of efficiency and his
unwavering faith in data-driven solutions, had spent countless
rotations studying the intricacies of Jacksonian metabolism. His
pioneering work in bio-engineered fungi cultivation had, for a
time, solved their previous dietary crisis, leading to the creation
of Fungihsonville, the orbital station that housed their carefully
curated ecosystem of edible fungi.

But even the most meticulously planned systems are susceptible
to unforeseen variables.

The Jacksons, for all their advanced technology and interstellar
wisdom, had a rather...unfortunate Achilles' heel. Their digestive systems, while capable of processing a bewildering array of
organic compounds, were notoriously sensitive to unfamiliar

6

bacteria. This presented a rather significant obstacle when it came to exploring new culinary horizons.

Direct contact with sentient species, even for the purpose of a friendly inquiry about the potential palatability of their flesh, was strictly forbidden by the Non-Interference Agreement, a cornerstone of Jacksonian ethics. This left them with a rather limited menu of options when it came to diversifying their diet. Procuring biological samples from deceased individuals for scientific research, however, was deemed perfectly acceptable.

Marvin, ever the pragmatist, saw an opportunity within these ethical constraints. When reports of a subtle but persistent decline in Jacksonian health began circulating through the network, he immediately initiated a new research project. He requisitioned tissue samples from a variety of deceased organisms, carefully cataloguing their nutritional content and analyzing their compatibility with Jacksonian physiology.

His lab, a model of efficiency and sterility, hummed with the low thrum of advanced analytical equipment. Holographic displays flickered with genetic sequences, molecular diagrams, and complex equations. Marvin, his brow furrowed in concentration, scrutinized the data streams, his three-fingered hands manipulating the controls with a practised ease.

It was during one of these late-night analysis sessions that Marvin stumbled upon a data point that would send ripples of both curiosity and unease through the Jacksonian network.

The subject of his current scrutiny wasn't a particularly exotic species of algae or a newly discovered strain of subterranean fungi, but a rather...unremarkable organism from a planet designated as Earth.

Marvin, his multifaceted eyes gleaming with a newfound intensity, activated a telepathic connection to the planetary network. "Colleagues," he announced, his voice a calm, steady frequency that resonated in the minds of every Jackson on Jacksonsonville, "I believe I've found a solution to our nutritional dilemma."

"It all began quite innocently, you see," Marvin had explained in a public broadcast. "We'd been analyzing the composition of various deceased organisms, strictly for research purposes, of course. Nothing untoward, purely a matter of due diligence before introducing any new food source to our delicate ecosystem."

"My latest analysis," he announced, "focused on a rather... unremarkable species from a planet designated as Earth. They call themselves 'humans'."

A holographic image of a human, meticulously rendered from Marvin's scans, materialized above the central console in his lab. The Jacksons across the planet observed with detached curiosity. The human, with its soft, fleshy exterior and its rather inefficient bipedal locomotion, didn't appear particularly threatening or noteworthy.

But as Marvin delved deeper into the data, a startling pattern emerged, a series of correlations that defied their initial expectations.

"The humans," he'd announced, his normally calm telepathic voice tinged with a flicker of excitement, "possess a remarkably high concentration of a particular protein that appears to have a synergistic effect with our existing dietary regime. In simpler terms, my colleagues, they're a nutritional wonder."

Within nanorotations, Marvin's announcement had circulated throughout the Jacksonian network, triggering a surge of data requests and analytical inquiries. Holographic displays across the planet flickered with cross-referenced data streams, population statistics, and projections of potential nutritional benefits.

Adhering to the Jacksons' strict ethical guidelines, Marvin's team conducted the initial trials using a limited supply of ethically procured human tissue. They developed a prototype food product — a spherical, protein-rich composite, meticulously calibrated for optimal Jacksonian digestion. The trials involved a controlled group of volunteer subjects, with comprehensive monitoring of their physiological responses, energy levels, and cognitive function. Preliminary analyses of the data exceeded expectations, indicating a 97.8% compatibility rate with existing metabolic pathways.

Further analysis of the trial data revealed an unexpected benefit: the human-derived meatball exhibited a 99.2% digestibility rate, even among Jacksonian subjects with a history of gastrointestinal sensitivity.

Marvin, encouraged by the positive trial results and the network's evident interest, began to formulate a comprehensive plan. He envisioned a system of controlled cultivation, meticulously designed to maximize the nutritional benefits of human-derived meatballs while adhering to the Jacksons' strict ethical guidelines.

He projected a detailed proposal onto the network, his holographic diagrams and data streams illuminating countless screens across Jacksonsonville. "Colleagues," he addressed the assembly, his telepathic voice resonating with calm confidence, "Imagine a future where our energy levels are consistently optimal, where digestive discomfort is a distant memory, where our physical vitality matches our intellectual prowess. The solution, I believe, lies in the sustainable and ethically sound utilization of human-derived nutrients."

This proposition, however, did not trigger a wave of universal approval. Subtle ripples of unease and dissent began to emerge within the network, a counterpoint to the prevailing current of pragmatic acceptance.

Grag Jackson, his brow furrowed as he reviewed the data streams pulsing through the network, felt a growing sense of unease. The proposed solution, while logically sound and seemingly efficient, triggered a cascade of warning signals within his meticulously organized mind.

Grag, a researcher renowned for his cautious nature and his unwavering adherence to the Precautionary Principle, had devoted his long lifespan to the study of other species. He'd meticulously documented countless examples of sentient life across the galaxy, each with its own unique evolutionary trajectory, its own complex set of behaviors, its own balance between instinct and consciousness.

The humans, however, presented a series of anomalies that defied Grag's attempts at categorization. His long-range observations, meticulously documented over countless rotations, revealed a species seemingly driven by self-destructive impulses. They constructed sprawling cities that choked their atmosphere with noxious fumes, engaged in violent conflicts over abstract ideologies, and exhibited an insatiable hunger for material possessions that offered no discernible evolutionary advantage. Their actions, when analyzed through the lens of Jacksonian logic, were a paradox, a chaotic equation with no apparent solution.

Grag acknowledged the patterns, the meticulously documented evidence of their self-destructive behavior. He knew that the sum of their knowledge, while impressive, was dwarfed by the vast expanse of the unknown. Their understanding of the universe, of life itself, was a perpetually evolving, each new discovery revealing threads they had yet to imagine. Grag, for all his years of research, recognized the inherent limitations of their methods.

Was it possible, he wondered, that their current understanding of sentience was simply inadequate when applied to such a perplexing species? Could their methods of observation and analysis, so effective for categorizing other life forms, be missing a crucial dimension of the human experience? To base such a momentous decision solely on their current, admittedly limited, understanding felt...reckless.

"Marvin, my esteemed colleague," Grag had countered in a public broadcast, his thoughts pulsing with a soft amber light of concern, "while I admire your ingenuity, I believe we must proceed with caution. The humans, for all their flaws, may possess a level of sentience that we have yet to fully comprehend. To consume them without a thorough understanding of their nature would be a grave ethical transgression, a stain on our collective conscience."

Grag's cautionary note resonated through the network, triggering a cascade of analytical inquiries and counter-arguments. Holographic displays flickered with data streams, philosophical treatises, and historical precedents, as the Jacksons engaged in a planet-wide debate. Could sentience be definitively measured? Was it a function of logical processing power, the ability to communicate complex ideas, or something more elusive, something that defied their current understanding?

The Jacksons, for all their mastery of science and technology, had yet to fully unravel the enigma of consciousness. They could deconstruct the building blocks of matter, manipulate the flow of energy, and chart the course of celestial bodies with impeccable precision. But the origin and nature of consciousness remained a persistent mystery.

The debate raged on, splitting the Jacksonian community into factions. The pragmatists, led by Marvin, argued for expediency. The humans were a resource, plain and simple, a solution to a pressing problem. The precautionary principle advocates, spearheaded by Grag, urged caution. They demanded a deeper understanding of human nature before making a decision that could have irreversible consequences.

Caught in the crossfire of this ethical storm were the children of Jacksonsonville. The Jacksons, unlike humans, did not reproduce through biological means. They were a product of advanced bio-engineering, their consciousness nurtured in specialized incubation chambers. The process was meticulous, ensuring that each new generation inherited the accumulated wisdom and knowledge of their predecessors.

However, this process was also energy-intensive, requiring a steady supply of nutrients to fuel the incubation chambers and to sustain the developing consciousnesses. The Jacksons' traditional diet, based primarily on a species of highly intelligent fungi, had served them well for centuries. But the recent discovery of the fungi's potential sentience, coupled with the gradual decline in the Jacksons' physical capabilities, had forced them to seek alternative sources of nourishment.

Marvin's initial research was conducted with the utmost respect for the Non-Interference Agreement, he had relied on ethically acquired human remains. But the promising results of his meatball trials had sparked a new line of inquiry. The reliance on deceased individuals, he realized, presented a logistical bottleneck. Decomposition, while a fascinating natural process, was hardly conducive to the efficient, large-scale production of high-quality foodstuffs.

The solution, as Marvin saw it, was a simple matter of optimization. Why wait for nature's inefficient decomposition process when they possessed the technology to cultivate human tissue directly? Why rely on the limited supply of ethically acquired remains when a vast, self-replenishing source was readily available just a few light-years away? The question, posed to the Jacksonian network with a detached, almost clinical curiosity, was this: Could their ethical framework, so carefully crafted to guide their interactions with other species, accommodate such a...pragmatic approach?

The Jacksons Institute of Childcare, became a battleground for this ethical war. Some caregivers, convinced by Marvin's arguments, embraced the human meatball solution with pragmatic zeal. They saw it as a necessary sacrifice, a means to an end, a way to ensure the well-being of their own children, even if it meant the demise of another species.

Others, swayed by Grag's concerns, resisted this new dietary regime with a fierce protectiveness. They argued that the Jacksons, as a species that valued compassion and wisdom, could not in good conscience condone the consumption of sentient beings. They pointed to the children's increasing telepathic sensitivity, their growing awareness of the interconnectedness of all life, as evidence that the Jacksons were evolving beyond the need for such a morally questionable solution.

The debate, conducted entirely through the silent hum of their interconnected network, continued to simmer. The Jacksons observed earth more keenly, with a detached curiosity, their collective mind struggling to reconcile the humans' chaotic and often contradictory actions with their own understanding of logic, efficiency, and evolutionary principles.

Krook Jackson, the president of the Academy, had been observing the unfolding debate rather dully. From his office atop the Academy's central spire, he had access to every data stream, every whispered argument, every flicker of uncertainty within the network. He found the whole situation rather...tiresome. The Jacksons, for all their intellectual prowess, had a tendency to overthink even the simplest of matters.

"Well, now then," Krooks drawled in a public address, "aren't we in a right pickle? Seems like our esteemed colleagues are having a bit of a moral meltdown over a bunch of...well, let's just say they're not exactly the sharpest tools in the cosmic shed, are they? Running about in circles, covering themselves in bits of brightly colored fabric, shouting at each other about things that don't even exist. Honestly, it's enough to make you wonder if they've got a loose wire or two up there, in that...what do they call it? Ah yes, the 'brain'."

Krook paused, allowing his sarcasm to hang in the air. He found it rather ironic, the Jacksons agonizing over the ethics of consuming a species that seemed hell-bent on consuming itself. But, of course, as president of the Academy, he had to maintain a certain level of decorum, at least publicly. Privately, however, he couldn't resist a little telepathic chuckle at the sheer absurdity of it all.

"Now, don't get me wrong, colleagues," he continued, his voice dripping with faux-sincerity, "I'm all for ethical considerations. We wouldn't want to be accused of being...well, you know... gastronomically challenged, would we? But let's not lose sight of the bigger picture, shall we? Our resources are dwindling.

Our young ones are getting a bit... fragile, shall we say? And here we have this... abundant supply of... nutrients, just ripe for the taking. Seems like a perfectly logical solution to me. But then again, what do I know? I'm just a humble chairman, shackled to this administrative post, burdened with the tedious task of guiding you lot towards enlightenment."

Krook's address, broadcast across the network with a calculated blend of logic and subtle persuasion, shifted the tide of the debate. The anxieties of those who had expressed concern about the ethical implications of consuming humans were quickly overshadowed by a wave of pragmatic acceptance. The data, after all, was compelling.

Marvin, emboldened by the collective shift towards acceptance, expanded his research efforts. He established a dedicated team of geneticists, bio-engineers, and nutritionists, tasked with optimizing the cultivation process and developing a range of human-derived food products that would meet the diverse dietary needs of the Jacksonian population. The results, meticulously documented and disseminated across the network, only reinforced the practicality of his solution.

On Earth, billions of humans went about their lives, oblivious to the fact that their very existence was being debated by a committee of highly evolved aliens with a fondness for data analysis and a rather unsettling approach to dietary planning. Their routines, their conflicts, their triumphs and tragedies — all meticulously documented, analyzed, and categorized by the Jacksons. Some humans, those who happened to be particularly high in protein or possessed a desirable omega-3 fatty acid profile, might have

16

felt a slight chill, a cosmic shiver down their spines. But for the most part, they remained blissfully unaware, continuing to play out the messy, illogical symphony of their existence, blissfully ignorant of the fact that their fate hung in the balance.

2

The Paradox of Human Fashion

The Jacksons were rather proud of their robes. In fact, the robe was seen as the pinnacle of their cultural innovation. Not because it was fancy—heavens, no. The Jacksons were a practical lot, and practicality was their guiding star. The robes they wore were a symbol of everything they held dear: simplicity, comfort, and a perfect balance between form and function. You see, the Jacksons had long concluded that clothing was, at its very core, a way to enhance one's ability to exist in harmony with their surroundings. It kept the methane-rich atmosphere out of one's eyes and didn't get in the way when they needed to access one of their myriad pockets for a snack or tool.

For centuries, the Jacksons had quietly congratulated themselves on what they considered the ideal relationship between life and fabric. They had hit the proverbial nail on the head when it came to attire, or so they thought. The robe was practical. It was purely about living life in a way that was efficient, balanced, and without any fuss. The very idea of clothing that wasn't purely functional was so foreign, so absurd to the Jacksons, that when they first encountered humans, it nearly broke their collective minds.

To put it simply, they were bulldozed by the human approach to clothing. They hadn't expected to find a species wearing anything at all, let alone entire wardrobes of bizarre and re-strictive garments. The Jacksons had assumed they were alone in figuring out how to incorporate clothing into their daily existence. But then came the humans, draped in layers upon layers of impractical materials, colours that served no apparent purpose, and cuts that seemed more like a hazard to movement than an aid to it.

Jacksonian scholars were dumbfounded. There was an entire species that didn't just wear clothes for comfort but seemed to make it an entire cultural phenomenon. Clothes for warmth? Sure, that made sense. Clothes for protection? Logical. But clothes that served neither purpose and instead squeezed, pinched, and at times suffocated their wearers? That was pure madness. The Jacksons were puzzled and, quite frankly, horrified. They gathered in their great halls, robes swirling in the ever-calm breeze of their methane atmosphere, to ponder what they had witnessed.

To the Jacksons, who conducted their lives in airy, climate-controlled comfort beneath the gentle warmth of their sun, the human predilection for heavy fabrics and constricting layers seemed an act of self-inflicted discomfort. On Jacksonsonville, where the average temperature hovered around a pleasant 88 Jacksonn degrees (a comfortable 12.8 degrees Celsius for the

Earth-minded), the very idea of a human enduring a suit and tie was enough to elicit bewilderment across their telepathic network.

During one of their communal gatherings, a group of Jacksons, including Grag, Marvin, and the wise Quait Jackson from the academy, engaged in a spirited debate about this human oddity. The Gathering Hall hummed with a low thrum of telepathic energy as Jacksons from across the city connected, their thoughts intermingling like the delicate strands of a luminous web. Holographic projections shimmered in the air, displaying scenes from Grag's research — humans in suits, sweating profusely under a blazing sun, their faces contorted in a grimace of discomfort that was both perplexing and comical to the observing Jacksons.

"Why would they subject themselves to such discomfort?" Grag pondered aloud, his thoughts rippling across the network. "It defies all logic and understanding of comfort."

Marvin, always looking to add a health perspective, chimed in, "Perhaps it's a form of endurance training? Testing their bodies' limits in extreme conditions? Though, I must admit, it does seem counterproductive to their well-being."

Quait Jackson, who had always been fascinated by the intricacies of different cultures, offered another view. "Could it not be a cultural ritual of some sort? A display of status or adherence to social norms, perhaps? We have seen similar, albeit less extreme, practices in other sentient species."

20

The debate continued, with various Jacksons offering theories ranging from heat-endurance rituals to bizarre fashion trends driven by unseen social forces. A young Jackson named Jax, known for his inquisitive nature and his love for spending his free time meticulously categorizing various species of bioluminescent lichen, raised a point.

"What if their clothing isn't just about physical comfort?" Jax chimed in, his thoughts tinged with the green luminescence of his latest lichen discovery. "What if it's more about social comfort or identity? We Jacksons have our robes, which are perfectly adapted to our environment. Perhaps their suits and dresses are adapted to their *social* environment?"

The idea struck a chord with many of the Jacksons. It was a perspective they hadn't considered—that human behavior could be influenced by factors beyond mere physical comfort.

"Jax may be onto something," Grag acknowledged, projecting images of human social gatherings onto the holographic display that shimmered at the center of the Hall. Images flickered—business meetings in towering structures of metal and glass, lavish celebrations in grand halls adorned with dazzling lights. The stark contrast in attire across different events and environments seemed to support the idea of clothing as a social tool.

"It's almost as if their clothing is a form of non-verbal communication," Jax observed. "A way to express unspoken rules, hierarchy, and even personal beliefs."

Marvin, scratching his chin thoughtfully, added, "It's a complex trade-off, then. They endure physical discomfort for what they perceive as social gain or acceptance. Intriguing, but still quite irrational from a health standpoint."

Grag nodded, his expression thoughtful. "This adds another layer to the complexity of human behavior. They're willing to endure discomfort, even harm, to adhere to these unspoken social codes. It's a peculiar prioritization of social conformity over individual well-being."

The Jacksons, having thoroughly explored various aspects of human clothing behavior, ultimately gravitated towards a consensus that underscored the irrationality of humans. The cultural explanations, while intriguing, did not seem sufficient to justify what they viewed as the significant discomfort and impracticality humans often endured for the sake of social norms.

Quait, summing up the sentiment of the group, projected a series of images showcasing elaborate human costumes, some so cumbersome they hindered basic movement. "Despite our attempts to understand this from a cultural perspective," he stated, his thoughts tinged with a lavender hue of puzzlement, "it seems increasingly clear that humans engage in practices that are fundamentally irrational. They knowingly sacrifice comfort, health, and even environmental sustainability for the sake of social conformity."

After the discussion in the Gathering Hall, an esteemed Jacksonian sociologist, Kruma Jackson, published a groundbreaking paper on their planet's all-pervasive social media platform. The paper, titled "The Irrationality of Human Attire: An Exploration of Earth's Peculiar Customs," quickly became a hot topic of discussion among the Jacksons.

Kruma's paper was a scintillating mix of sharp wit, profound insights, and a touch of playful sarcasm that captivated the Jacksonian audience. She began by highlighting the numerous instances where humans seemingly disregarded their comfort, health, and practicality for the sake of fashion.

"Consider the phenomenon of 'high heels,'" Kruma wrote, projecting an image of a human precariously balanced on footwear that seemed more suited for a tightrope walker than daily life. "Humans, particularly of the female variety, subject themselves to this torturous practice, wobbling on these stilts that could very well be instruments of mild torture."

She then delved into the realm of formal wear, questioning the logic behind suits and ties in sweltering heat. "Imagine, if you will," she wrote, accompanying her words with a humorous animation of a group of Jacksons attempting to navigate a sauna while clad in stiff suits and choking on neckties, "a group of humans gathering under the blistering sun, cloaked in layers of fabric, choking themselves with decorative nooses called 'ties.' It's a spectacle of voluntary discomfort!"

Kruma's argument wasn't limited to everyday fashion. She explored extreme examples, like the heavy, elaborate costumes worn at the annual Earth festival they called "Carnaval," where humans adorned themselves in feathers, sequins, and head-dresses that seemed to defy all laws of physics and common sense. "At times, their attire is so cumbersome and elaborate, it impedes basic movement," Kruma observed. "Yet, they parade around joyously, as if in a trance of irrationality."

The paper didn't stop at merely critiquing human fashion. Kruma ventured into a more controversial territory, connecting the dots between human irrationality in clothing and the ethical implications of consuming human meatballs.

"If humans demonstrate such a blatant disregard for their own well-being and comfort," Kruma argued, "can we truly consider them rational beings worthy of the ethical considerations we extend to other species? Their nonsensical attire might just be an indication of a broader pattern of irrationality that questions the premise of treating them as equals in the cosmic hierarchy."

Grag Jackson, amidst the swirling discussions on Jackson-sonville, found himself at a crossroads. His research into human behavior had opened a Pandora's box of moral and ethical questions that he couldn't easily dismiss. While he couldn't fathom the human choice of clothing and continued to see it as irrational, he began to question the broader implications of their treatment.

The debate initiated by Kruma Jackson's paper on human attire had inadvertently steered the conversation towards the ethical consumption of humans. Grag, though perplexed by human customs, started to feel a growing unease about their commod-ification. He wondered if their downright irrational behavior regarding clothing justified the lack of welfare consideration.

In a series of introspective public broadcasts, Grag shared his conflicting thoughts with the Jacksonian network, his thoughts pulsing with uncertainty. "While I remain baffled by the human choice of clothing," he admitted, "it has dawned on me that our understanding of their culture and cognition is limited. Does this uncertainty not warrant a precautionary approach in how we treat them?"

3

The Scales of Sentience

By the year 2033, a subtle but significant shift had begun to manifest in the carefully calibrated consciousness of Jacksonsonville. The human meatball debate, once a mere murmur in their telepathic network, had taken on a new urgency. Something was happening to the children. Something that had even the most logically-minded Jacksons exchanging bewildered chirps of concern.

It began with seemingly innocuous anecdotes from the incubation chambers of the Jackson Institute of Childcare. Caregivers reported a heightened sensitivity among the youngsters who had been weaned on a diet of human meatballs. Their telepathic transmissions, usually as clear and predictable as a data stream, were now tinged with an unexpected intensity.

Linna Jackson, barely four rotations old, startled his caregiver by suddenly declaring, "The Zorposed is feeling anxious. He misses his mate."

Now, Linna, while a bright spark, had never exhibited any particular affinity for the Zorposed, the elephant-like creatures who roamed the carefully preserved savannas of Jacksonsonville. Her interests usually revolved around categorizing bioluminescent fungi and perfecting his technique for crafting algae sculptures.

The caregiver, initially skeptical, telepathically contacted the Zorposed in question (as one does in a society where direct mind-to-mind communication is as commonplace as texting is to humans). To her astonishment, Linna's assessment was spot on. The Zorposed *was* indeed experiencing a wave of loneliness, pining for his mate who was currently on a migration route to the northern polar regions.

Similar stories began to surface across the network. Children who had indulged in human meatballs were displaying an uncanny ability to sense the emotions of other species, even at a distance. Their telepathic acuity, already impressive by Jacksonian standards, had seemingly been amplified.

Marvin Jackson, whose research had inadvertently unleashed this telepathic awakening, pored over the data with professional pride. He'd always been driven by a desire to improve the health and well-being of his people. The initial experiments with human meatballs, conducted with ethically procured samples, had pointed to a promising solution to their nutritional dilemma.

But now, faced with the unexpected consequences, a whole new set of variables had entered the equation.

"The evidence is clear, my dear colleagues," Marvin announced in a network-wide broadcast. "Human protein has a demonstrable effect on our telepathic abilities, particularly in developing minds. But the mechanism, the long-term implications... well, those are still under investigation."

Marvin's announcement, cautiously worded as it was, threw Jacksonsonville into a state of heightened excitement (and, in some quarters, a good dose of telepathic indigestion).

The companies that had been experimenting with human-based food products seized upon this news with entrepreneurial zeal. Frozen human meatball packs flew off the shelves of the bio-markets. Marketing campaigns, projecting shimmering holographic images of children beaming with telepathic energy, flooded the network. Self-proclaimed gurus, their iridescent robes radiating the promise of enlightenment (and a hefty profit margin), sprang up like bioluminescent mushrooms after a methane rain, offering workshops and seminars on how to harness the "human essence" for maximum telepathic potential.

Brew Jackson, a young universitarian whose flamboyant pronouncements and audacious theories had already made him a bit of a celebrity on Jacksonsonville, seized upon this moment with the zeal of a meteor streaking towards a black hole. Brew, a captivating blend of charisma and enthusiasm, was conducting his doctoral studies in a rather unusual field: the intersection of astrophysics and spirituality. He saw the human meatball phenomenon as confirmation of his own cosmically-inclined theories.

My fellow Jacksons," Brew projected, his thoughts a ripple of excitement across the network, "we stand at the precipice of a profound discovery. The human essence, it appears, holds a key to unlocking deeper levels of our own telepathic potential.

He paced his stage, his flamboyant robes swirling around him like a nebula in motion. "The human essence," he proclaimed, his voice rising to a theatrical crescendo, "is a catalyst, a portal, a key to unlocking the hidden potential within us all! By consuming this...unique form of nourishment, we will embrace the potential to syncronizing into the universal flow! "

He paused, letting the implications sink in. "Imagine, a heightened awareness, an interconnectedness beyond anything we've ever known. The human meatballs offer us a chance to explore the very limits of our telepathic abilities."

Brew's pronouncements, had a profound effect on Jacksonsonville. Some embraced his message with fervent enthusiasm, eagerly joining the ranks of the meatball movement. Others remained skeptical, clinging to their traditional values and questioning the ethical implications of consuming another sentient being.

The universe, in its infinite capacity for generating awkward situations, had presented the Jacksons with a choice: embrace the telepathic boost or face the existential dread of realizing their favorite snack might be having an existential crisis.

Despite the swell of excitement — or perhaps *because* of it — Grag Jackson felt a surge of unease ripple through his very being. He

29

observed the growing fervor surrounding human meatballs, the increasingly audacious pronouncements of Brew, and the children's burgeoning telepathic abilities with a disquiet that wouldn't be soothed by logic alone.

Marvin's call for caution resonated deeply with him. The Jacksons, in their long history, had always adhered to a principle that guided their every decision, a principle so deeply ingrained in their collective consciousness that it was as natural as breathing their methane-rich air: the Precautionary Principle.

During a somber address broadcasted across the network, Grag explained, his thoughts radiating a soft amber glow of unwavering conviction, "My esteemed colleagues, in our pursuit of progress, in our quest for understanding, let us not forget the wisdom of our ancestors. They have bequeathed unto us a guiding star, a principle that has preserved the harmony of our existence for millennia: the Precautionary Principle."

Holographic projections flickered into existence around him, displaying scenes from Jacksonian history—the careful terraforming of their planet, the ethical guidelines for their bioengineering advancements, the protocols for interspecies interaction.

"This principle, my friends, is not merely a rule, it's woven into the very fabric of our being. It's the voice of caution whispering in our ears when we contemplate any action with uncertain consequences. It's the quiet hum of prudence that guides our hand when we wield the power to reshape our reality."

He continued, his voice a soothing baritone that resonated across the network, "Imagine a young Jacksonian, brimming with curiosity, eager to explore the properties of a newly discovered algae strain. They could, of course, simply ingest it, observe the effects, and document the results. But what if this new strain contains an unforeseen toxin? What if it disrupts our digestive systems, clouds our telepathic clarity, or introduces a novel pathogen into our meticulously balanced ecosystem?"

"This," Grag stressed, his thoughts pulsing with a gentle but persistent urgency, "is where the Precautionary Principle comes into play. It dictates that we proceed with caution, with meticulous observation, with thorough analysis *before* we commit to a course of action that could have unintended consequences."

He projected a new set of images onto the holographic screens — charts, diagrams, and genetic sequences showcasing the complexities of human biology. "The human meatball dilemma presents us with an unprecedented level of uncertainty. We've seen the potential benefits, the increased telepathic abilities in our young ones. But we've also witnessed unsettling events — those erratic societal responses on Earth following our recent experiment."

Grag's thoughts shifted to a deeper shade of amber, reflecting the weight of his concern. "We have not yet definitively determined whether or not these humans are sentient beings. To act without certainty, to proceed with a harvesting program before we fully understand the consequences for *them*, would be a grave violation of our ethical principles."

His address concluded with a plea for patience and continued research. "Let us not rush into this, colleagues. Let us not be swayed by fear or ambition, by the promise of enhanced abilities, or the anxieties of our present dilemma. The Precautionary Principle demands a meticulous and compassionate approach. We owe it to ourselves, to our future, and yes, even to these perplexing humans, to proceed with wisdom and restraint."

Grag's broadcast sent a calming wave through the Jacksonian network, but the tension remained palpable. The need for a solution, a sustainable and ethically sound solution, was more urgent than ever. The question of the human's sentience loomed large.

Brew, in response, crafted a characteristically spirited, yet academic, counter-argument. "Grag, my esteemed colleague, always the voice of reason and prudence," Brew's holographic image projected into countless living spaces, showcasing him in a meditative pose within a perfectly manicured bioluminescent garden. "But are we, perhaps, being a tad...overly cautious in this particular instance? A touch too generous with our application of the principle? After all, haven't we stumbled upon something remarkable here? Science has illuminated a path—the human essence offers tangible enhancement to our abilities!"

"Now, I do wholeheartedly agree that respecting sentience is paramount," Brew continued, leaning forward slightly, his eyes twinkling with a mischievous glint, "But what constitutes sentience? And are we, perhaps, being a tad inconsistent with our application of this principle? On one hand, we're agonizing over consuming *humans*, a species that, while undeniably perplexing, demonstrates a certain...disregard for the well-being of their planet and, quite frankly, for each other. And on the *other* hand, we have no qualms about harvesting our dear, delicious fungi for sustenance. And let's not even mention the poor algae, cheerfully bubbling away in their vats, contributing so selflessly to our dietary regime!."

He paused for a beat, letting his words resonate. "Now, don't misunderstand me, I'm not advocating for rampant, thoughtless consumption, " he said with a playful wave of his three-fingered tentacle. "I propose, my dear colleagues, that we establish a scale of sentience. A nuanced system that takes into account a species' actions, their impact on the universe, their demonstrable capacity for empathy and interconnectedness."

He conjured a holographic representation of a vertical scale, with "Algae" at the bottom, "Fungi" somewhere in the middle, and "Jacksons," of course, proudly perched at the top. "We've already seen through observation that human behaviour leaves much to be desired, ethically and environmentally. Where do *they* belong on this scale? What separates them from our delectable fungi? From the algae that sustains us? Why, in light of this extraordinary discovery, must we cling to the status quo? Is it not our duty to embrace progress, to allow science to illuminate the path toward a healthier and more vibrant Jacksonian society?"

Brew chuckled, a good-natured ripple of amusement coursing through the network. "Grag, my ever-so-wise colleague, has rightly emphasized the importance of the Precautionary

Principle. Let's not rush to any conclusions. Instead, let's ponder upon this Sentience Scale. Let's use our collective intellect, our shared knowledge, to determine the most ethical course of action."

"After all," he continued, his tone shifting to one of thoughtful inquiry, "as Marvin has pointed out, we still don't fully understand *why* human protein has such a profound effect on our young ones. The evidence is undeniable, but the underlying mechanisms remain elusive. My research, going forward, will delve deeper into these questions. Let's analyze the curious data, study these perplexing humans with Jacksonian diligence, and let our findings, not our assumptions, guide us towards a solution that upholds our values and ensures the well-being of all—be it Jackson, fungi, or yes, even these wonderfully weird humans."

4

Brew and Jax Chew the Fat

On the lush, bioluminescent grounds of Jacksonsonville University, Brew Jackson and Jax Jackson sat beneath a shimmering canopy of genetically engineered starlight orchids, their conversation meandering through the cosmos of outlandish ideas. Brew, radiating a vibrant, almost kinetic aura, and Jax, his thoughts pulsing with a quiet intensity, delved into the peculiarities of human behavior.

Brew, waving his hands expressively, launched into an offbeat analogy. "Jax, consider this—humans wear those tight, restrictive neckties, right? Now, what if these ties are actually subconscious antennas to the universe, trying to tune into cosmic frequencies, but they got it all wrong!"

Jax chuckled, his brow furrowed in playful thought. "And what if their obsession with footwear is actually an unconscious attempt to ground themselves to Earth's energy fields? They're constantly changing shoes, trying to find the right 'frequency'."

Brew, energized by the trajectory of their thoughts, added, "Yes, and every new fashion trend is like a new attempt at a ritual to harmonize with the planet! But they've forgotten the meaning, and now it's just a bizarre dance of fabric and color."

Jax, leaning forward with intrigue, tied it to their earlier discussion about human sustainability. "Imagine if their fashion cycles are a reflection of Earth's own environmental cycles," he mused, "like they're mimicking the seasons or the migration patterns of birds, but in a completely abstracted, human way."

Brew nodded enthusiastically. "Exactly! And this whole cycle of buying and discarding clothes could be an unconscious mimicry of Earth's renewal processes — like shedding leaves or regrowing forests, but in a twisted, humanized form."

Jax, his eyes twinkling with amusement, ventured further, "So, in a way, they're trying to connect with their planet but end up doing the exact opposite! It's like a cosmic joke they're not in on."

A gentle chime echoed in Brew's mind, momentarily interrupting his train of thought. "Ah, apologies, Jax," Brew chuckled, "that'll be my hydration reminder. Seems I'm due for a methane top-up."

He gestured towards a nearby kiosk, a sleek, bioluminescent dome pulsating with a soft, green glow. "Care to join me? I hear they've got a new batch of fermented algae extract. Surprisingly palatable, if you can get past the initial sulfurous bouquet."

Jax grinned. "Can't resist a good sulfurous bouquet. Lead the way."

The two Jacksons made their way towards the kiosk, their conversation punctuated by the gentle clicks and whirs of passing transport pods and the soft, melodic hum of the city's energy grid. As they sipped their algae extract, Brew's thoughts drifted back to the paradox of human behavior.

"You know, Jax," Brew mused, his gaze drawn to the swirling patterns of bioluminescent algae in his drink, "what if it's not just about fashion or habits? What if humans are actually controlled by some sort of cosmic artificial intelligence, and all this incoherence is just a bug in the system?"

Jax rubbed his chin thoughtfully. "A cosmic AI, huh? That explains a lot. Like why people are obsessed with capturing every moment on their phones. Maybe they're programmed to *document* life, not live it."

Brew's eyes lit up with fervor as he pondered Jax's remark. "Imagine, a cosmic AI, subtly guiding humanity's evolution, but somewhere along the line, there's a glitch. All these irrational behaviors, their fashion, their obsessions with technology, are symptoms of this malfunction."

Jax nodded, intrigued by the direction of their conversation. "It's as if humans are trapped in a loop, continuously repeating patterns that no longer serve a purpose, yet they can't break free. It's like watching a program running amok, devoid of its original intent."

Brew, always keen on exploring spiritual realms, speculated further. "What if this AI was initially programmed to help humans achieve a higher state of consciousness, to connect more deeply with their planet? But now, it's lost control, and humans are spiraling into chaos."

Jax leaned back, absorbing the enormity of the hypothesis. "That would mean their entire civilization is a grand experiment, a test of whether a species can overcome its programming and find its way back to cosmic harmony."

The conversation then shifted back to the ethical dilemma surrounding the consumption of human meatballs. Brew, with a contemplative expression, said, "This cosmic AI hypothesis, if true, brings a new perspective to our ethical debate. Are we consuming beings that are essentially lost in a cosmic error? Does that make our actions more justifiable, or does it compel us to show even greater empathy?"

Jax pondered for a moment before responding. "If humans are indeed victims of a cosmic glitch, it adds a layer of complexity to our moral responsibility. Perhaps our role isn't just about dietary choices but also about aiding a species that's inadvertently strayed from its evolutionary path."

Brew, his eyes reflecting a mix of revelation and resolution, responded firmly, "If humans are merely the byproducts of a cosmic AI's programming gone awry, they're akin to robots, mere puppets of a higher system. Their so-called consciousness might just be an advanced level of programming, not genuine sentience."

He continued, his tone shifting to one of lighthearted obser-vation, "Think about it, Jax. Humans put themselves in large metal boxes, rush around at high speeds, and then complain about not having enough time. They create complex gadgets to save time, only to waste it staring at smaller glowing screens."

Jax, laughing, joined in. "And their obsession with capturing images of their meals! They don't just eat; they need to document the eating process, as if the meal's existence depends on its digital footprint."

Brew, shaking his head in amusement, added, "Contrast that with the zoopards. Now, *there's* a species that knows how to live. They bask in the sun, they play in the fields, and when they eat, it's a straightforward affair. No gadgets, no rush, just living in the moment."

Jax, still chuckling, said, "The zoopards have an uncomplicated wisdom. They understand their place in the ecosystem. They don't build unsustainable structures or create needless waste. They live in perfect harmony with their environment."

Brew, adopting a mock-serious tone, continued, "And let's not forget their communication. No need for complex languages or misinterpretations. A simple series of chirps and tail wags, and they understand each other perfectly."

Jax, nodding in agreement, added, "Yes, and they don't wear restrictive clothing or follow bizarre trends. Their fur changes with the seasons, naturally adapting to their needs. It's the epitome of practicality and elegance."

As the iridescent glow of the starlight orchids shifted from emerald to sapphire, signaling the approaching dawn, Brew and Jax finished their fermented algae extract, the sulfurous aftertaste lingering like a philosophical afterthought.

"It's fascinating, Jax," Brew said, his voice tinged with a renewed sense of wonder. "No matter how we try to rationalize it, human behavior remains a labyrinth of illogical actions. They engage in practices that seemingly serve no purpose or benefit to their well-being."

Jax, equally perplexed, added, "Indeed, Brew. Their actions often contradict their self-interest. Take their environmental policies, for instance. Despite clear evidence of harm, they continue behaviors that damage their own planet."

Brew, leaning in, his brow furrowed with a mix of concern and curiosity, said, "And that's just the tip of the iceberg. Their social structures, filled with contradictions and inefficiencies, are a maze of confusion. It's as if they're following a script that's devoid of any coherent narrative."

Jax, with a thoughtful nod, replied, "This puzzling nature of human behavior strengthens our argument for choosing human meatballs over fungi. Our fungi are a harmonious part of our ecosystem, while humans disrupt their own. In a strange way, our consumption of human meatballs is a lesser ethical dilemma compared to the potential disruption of our ecological balance."

Brew, contemplating the precautionary principle, added, "That's true, Jax. Our choice, though unconventional, is made with careful consideration of the impacts. We're treading a path guided by caution and a respect for life, constantly reevaluating our decisions as we gain more understanding."

Jax, acknowledging their limited understanding, said, "Exactly. Our decision to consume human meatballs isn't a dismissal of human life but an acknowledgment of our current understanding of their nature. We stay vigilant and open to new information that could change our perspective."

Brew, with a sense of duty, concluded, "Our journey as a species is one of exploration and moral questioning. We must navigate these ethical waters with care, respecting the complex tapestry of life in the cosmos, even when it defies our understanding."

As the night gave way to the first light of dawn, Brew and Jax ended their dialogue with a renewed sense of their ethical responsibilities. Their conversation, a blend of curiosity and philosophical inquiry, echoed the Jacksons' commitment to exploring the unknown while maintaining a deep respect for all forms of life, no matter how enigmatic or incomprehensible they might appear.

5

The Evolution

One might ask how the Jacksons had attained such high levels of development, enabling their exploration of other planets. Surely, they must have undergone various phases of growth and societal progression. However, the Jacksons' evolutionary process was both similar and dissimilar to that of Earth's humans. Evolving on a different planet, all life forms on Jacksonsonville descended from a single organism. Over millions of years, a species destined to become the Jacksons chose a suitable spot in the Via Lactea to establish their society, away from nearby life forms, creating a world focused solely on themselves—Jacksonsonville.

From the beginning, the Jacksons possessed a highly intelligent consciousness, capable of telepathic communication. Their societal foundation was grounded in cooperation and philosophical exploration, aimed not at power but at improving their lifestyle. They recognized the lesser intelligent creatures coexisting on their planet, offering assistance and learning to respect their way of life.

From their inception on Jacksonsonville, the Jacksons possessed a natural inclination for telepathic communication and collaboration. These abilities, ingrained in their essence, formed the bedrock of their society. They developed a community where philosophical and ethical discussions were not just pastimes but integral to their way of life, constantly striving to improve their collective existence.

The Jacksons breathed a composition rich in hydrogen — a lightweight and plentiful gas that coursed through their bodies, reacting within specialized cells to release the energy essential for sustaining their advanced cerebral functions and telepathic communications. Instead of burning this energy, a complex chain of reactions harnessed it.

Helium, filling the spaces between hydrogen molecules, played a crucial role in the Jacksons' physiology. Although it didn't chemically react, helium's presence ensured the integrity of their cellular membranes, providing stability amidst the fluctuating pressures and temperatures of their atmospheric home. This delicate equilibrium was necessary for the Jacksons' intricate biological processes.

Methane underwent disassembly and reconfiguration within their bodies, with its carbon forming the backbone of complex organic molecules. Ammonia, carrying vital nitrogen, intricately wove itself into the fabric of their beings, constructing proteins that formed their telepathic organs and sustained the delicate balance of their internal ecosystems.

Water vapor, suspended in the atmosphere, was absorbed and meticulously utilized within their cells. Serving as a carrier of dissolved substances, a facilitator of metabolic reactions, and a regulator of their internal environments, water vapor ensured that the Jacksons' physiological systems operated with the precision and efficiency demanded by their highly developed society.

The Jacksons had developed a unique form of respiration, harmoniously aligned with the atmosphere of Jacksonville. Their existence revolved around a continuous cycle of inhaling and exhaling, an exchange with their very environment. This finely tuned alignment reflected the fact that Jacksonville had been carefully chosen as their home due to its exact quantities of natural resources that allowed the Jacksons to thrive. The ancestors of the Jacksons, who no longer maintained contact with their species, had chosen this planet for reasons unknown even to the Jacksons themselves, who had been exported to Jacksonville with highly evolved consciousness and telepathic abilities.

Their remarkable abilities made their way of life nearly unimaginable to outsiders. They could instantly absorb all provided knowledge, leading to little variety from Jackson to Jackson in terms of culturally acquired knowledge. This rapid knowledge absorption extended to their mastery of the planet's resources, nearly optimizing them to 100 percent levels, effectively eradicating social inequality. Their society thrived on individual choices, fostering profound philosophical and ethical discussions to determine the best way to lead their lives. With a life expectancy of 237 years, they held a deep sense of individual health.

Despite their small population of five million on Jacksonville, the Jacksons were highly social and could connect with one another willingly. They had developed spacecraft deeply in-grained with their telepathic abilities, allowing them to send capsules that connected to the operating Jackson, who could then teleport the capsule within a range of 500 light years from their planet. Their incredible manipulation of the environment included expertise in dark matter manipulation, enabling var-ious constructions. However, they adhered to a simple way of life, primarily using telepathic consciousness to transfer themselves and dispose of waste directly into space, ensuring optimal planetary sustenance.

Although they had different niches within their society, such as social gurus advocating for more spirituality, the Jacksons grappled primarily with questions of right and wrong, what is and what ought to be. They had deeply delved into finding a substitute for their fungi-based diet, as they believed it was unfair to the fungi. Their study of fungi consciousness had not yet yielded a consensus.

For reproduction, the Jacksons required the union of two in-dividuals, leading them to form monogamous relationships that typically endured throughout their lives. In the quest for the optimal relationship structure, they delved into various formations, grappling with the challenge of some Jacksons not adhering to monogamy. The debates raged on, centering around the options of open relationships versus closed ones.

Ultimately, they arrived at a profound conclusion, drawing from their collective wisdom and employing a rather conservative way of explanation to shed light on their choice. They understood that giving in to their inner urges for mingling with other Jacksons might offer short-term benefits but ultimately led to a long-term emptiness of being. On the other hand, closed relationships, though challenging, offered the potential for building a greater good—fostering love and trust between two Jacksons who would share their lives, collaborate on intergalactic journeys, and remain deeply connected to their Jacksons community.

The debates on relationship structures were as enduring as the dietary dilemma they had once faced. However, the Jacksons collectively agreed that monogamy was the superior way of life. It allowed them to escape the turmoil of infidelity and the sense of emptiness that a life of sharing with many had once caused. Through this consensus, they found a path that harmonized individual desires with the broader well-being of their society.

Coexistence with Native Species

As the Jacksons evolved on Jacksonsonville, they encountered various native species, each unique in its own right. Their approach to these beings was guided by principles that focused on what individuals are able to be and do.

The Zorposed, akin to Earth's elephants in their gentle nature and grand stature, roamed the plains of Jacksonsonville. The Jacksons, recognizing their intelligence and emotional depth, engaged with them not as dominators but as respectful cohabitants. They ensured that the Zorposed had ample space to thrive, understanding their need for social bonds and environmental enrichment.

Resembling the seals of Earth, the Gorpods were playful creatures that inhabited Jacksonsonville's oceans and rivers. The Jacksons admired their joyful nature and ensured their aquatic homes were kept pristine. Efforts were made to understand their communication patterns, allowing for a harmonious coexistence that respected the Gorpods' capabilities for play and social interaction.

The Truupods, similar to monkeys, were known for their curiosity and agility. The Jacksons observed their complex social structures and were careful not to disrupt their natural habitats. They fostered an environment where the Truupods could exercise their physical and cognitive abilities, ensuring their flourishing within the ecosystem.

Krupords, akin to dogs, formed close bonds with the Jacksons. These creatures were admired for their loyalty and emotional depth. The Jacksons provided them with care, companionship, and opportunities to engage in activities that catered to their natural instincts and social needs.

In their interactions with these species, the Jacksons' approach was not about utilizing these beings for the Jacksons' benefit but ensuring that they had the opportunity to live fulfilling lives according to their nature.

1. Life: The Jacksons ensured the safety and health of all species,

respecting their right to life.

2. Bodily Health: Adequate habitats and nutrition were maintained for each species.

3. Bodily Integrity: Each species was free from cruel treatment and exploitation.

4. Senses, Imagination, and Thought: The Jacksons encouraged the natural behavior and cognitive abilities of each species.

5. Emotions: The Jacksons recognized the emotional capacities of these beings, ensuring their mental well-being.

6. Practical Reason: The Jacksons respected the decision-making processes of these species within their societal structures.

7. Affiliation: The social structures and bonds within each species were honored and protected.

8. Other Species: The interdependence and relationships among different species were maintained in a balanced ecosystem.

9. Play: Opportunities for leisure and play were provided, recognizing their importance in the well-being of these beings.

10. Control over One's Environment: Each species had a degree of autonomy and control over their environment, ensuring their ability to thrive in their natural habitat.

Reflecting on Their Own Development

In understanding and implementing these principles, the Jacksons often reflected on their own evolutionary journey. They acknowledged that their ancestors had sent them to populate a world that was already teeming with life, each species minding its own business. As they co-evolved with these native beings, they chose an approach that was respectful and nurturing.

This approach led the Jacksons to ponder their unique evolution and development. Unlike humans, who evolved through various stages of societal and technological advancements often marred by conflict and exploitation, the Jacksons' evolution was more harmonious and cooperative. Their inherent telepathic abilities and cooperative nature had shielded them from many of the pitfalls that plagued human development.

However, this did not make the Jacksons complacent. They understood that their way of life was just one path among many. As they continued to learn and grow, they remained mindful of the broader implications of their actions, not only within their planet but also in their interactions with other worlds, including Earth. The ethical debates and philosophical discussions that formed the core of their society were a testament to their commitment to continual improvement and understanding.

6

Brew's Reflections

Brew Jackson paced restlessly in his study, the iridescent hues of his robes swirling around him like a nebula in turmoil. His brow was furrowed, his multifaceted eyes reflecting the flickering holographic projections that surrounded him. Leavens' latest research, detailing the human tendency to swathe themselves in layers of impractical fabrics even in sweltering heat, had left him utterly perplexed.

"It's baffling, Kruma—utterly baffling!" Brew exclaimed, his thoughts resonating with a frantic hum of confusion. He turned toward Kruma, who sat serenely on a plush cushion, her amethyst robes a calming counterpoint to his frenetic energy.

Kruma, ever the voice of reason, tilted her head, her eyes reflecting the swirling patterns of the holograms. "What's perplexing you this time, my love? Another human fashion show in the Sahara Desert?"

A chuckle rippled through Brew's mind. "Worse," he groaned, sinking into a chair beside her. "Leavens' paper quantifies the sheer waste they generate with their fashion cycles. They discard perfectly functional garments, replacing them with newer, equally impractical versions, season after season, year after year. It's a vortex of consumption with no apparent end in sight!"

Kruma's brow furrowed with concern. "It's a blatant disregard for resources," she agreed. "Their robes, unlike ours—which last a lifetime—seem to have built-in obsolescence. We've been together for forty-four rotations, and my robes are as vibrant and functional as the day we met in the nurseries." She smoothed the shimmering fabric of her sleeve, a subtle iridescent wave rippling across its surface. "To think, they exchange their entire wardrobes for no apparent reason, often acquiring garments entirely unsuited to their environments."

"And not only that," Brew added, his exasperation mounting, "their obsession with replacing perfectly functional gadgets with newer models, simply for the sake of novelty, is equally baffling. Imagine spending hours staring at a screen on a perfectly sunny day, only to discard the device a few months later for a slightly thinner, slightly shinier version. It's madness!"

Brew shuddered, imagining the mountains of discarded electronics piling up on Earth—a stark contrast to their own planet, where every atom of waste was meticulously recycled or dematerialized. "It's a level of consumption that defies any sense of logic or sustainability," he muttered. "They seem driven by an insatiable hunger for novelty, for the fleeting

51

satisfaction of acquiring the latest and greatest, with no regard for the long-term consequences."

"And the most perplexing aspect of it all," Kruma added, her thoughts tinged with a soft amethyst glow of frustration, "is that they know how to do better. They launch rockets into space, recycle some materials, even possess theoretical knowledge of a circular economy! And yet, they apply these principles so selectively, so inconsistently. It's as if they possess the knowledge but lack the will—or perhaps the very capacity—to act in accordance with it."

"What truly baffles me," she continued, leaning forward, her gaze intense, "is their waste disposal. They hoard it, they bury it, they let it pollute their world! It's so obvious, so simple to dematerialize it or launch it into space. We've been doing it for millennia on Jacksonsonville. Any non-reusable material from our robes, our algae farms, even our... well, let's just say our personal waste—is instantly dematerialized or repurposed. Why create something you can't sustainably dispose of? It's the very antithesis of a circular system."

Brew, his brow furrowed in thought, stared at a projection of Earth's overflowing landfills, his stomach churning with disgust. "Those mountains of waste," he murmured, his voice tinged with horrified fascination. "They just... leave it there. Plastics, metals, organic matter—all piling up, leaching toxins into their soil and water, poisoning their own nest. It's a form of self-destruction on a scale that's almost incomprehensible."

"It's a tragic betrayal of the very planet that sustains them,"

Kruma agreed. "And it's not just themselves they're harming. Think of the countless other species that share their world — the delicate ecosystems they're disrupting, the innocent creatures they're driving to extinction. It's a cascade of suffering, a ripple effect of destruction that extends far beyond their own species."

"You know, Kruma," Brew mused, "until I started researching humans, I'd never encountered a species that generated waste it couldn't fully reintegrate or safely dispose of. It seemed... well, unthinkable — a fundamental violation of the natural order. It's as if they've been programmed with a self-destruct sequence, a code that compels them to undermine their own existence."

A chilling thought struck Brew, sending a shiver down his iridescent spine. "Imagine," he whispered, "what it must be like for the other creatures on Earth. The squirrels, for instance — those small, furry beings who gather nuts and build their nests in the trees. They live simple lives, in tune with the natural rhythms of their world. And then, into their midst comes this... this glitch — a species that consumes and destroys everything in its path, a force of chaos that threatens to unravel the fabric of their existence."

He shuddered again, picturing a squirrel, its bright eyes wide with fear, darting for cover as a bulldozer roared through its forest home, leaving a trail of devastation in its wake. "What a horrifying reality that must be," he murmured, his voice filled with a profound sense of empathy for the countless creatures caught in the crossfire of human folly.

"It's a cosmic injustice," Kruma agreed, her amethyst eyes

reflecting a shared sense of sorrow. "And the most tragic aspect is that they seem oblivious to the suffering they inflict — both on themselves and on the other beings that share their planet. They continue to replicate, increasing their numbers, expanding their footprint, amplifying the very cycles of destruction that threaten to consume them all. It's a feedback loop of degradation, fueled by their insatiable appetite for more."

Brew, his mind ablaze with a newfound understanding, felt a surge of urgency coursing through him. He had to share this realization, this disturbing vision of human-induced suffering, with his fellow Jacksons.

"Kruma, my love," he said, his voice ringing with conviction, "I have to do a broadcast. The Jacksons need to hear this. They need to understand the true nature of the human dilemma — the ecological and ethical implications of their actions. This is not just about dietary choices; it's about our responsibility as a sentient species to act with compassion, to minimize suffering, to preserve the delicate balance of life."

Kruma, sensing the fire in his soul — the unshakable belief that burned within him — knew she couldn't hold him back. This was Brew at his most passionate, his most inspired, his most... Brew.

"Then do it, my love," she said gently. "Share your truth with the world. Let the Jacksons decide for themselves. But be careful, Brew. This is a dangerous path you're treading."

Brew, energized by Kruma's support, smiled, his eyes twinkling with a determined glint. "Don't worry, my dear. I wouldn't have it any other way."

He turned toward his workstation, his fingers dancing across the controls, activating the Jacksonian network. It was time for a broadcast. Time to stir the cosmic consciousness, to inject a dose of unsettling reality into the Jacksonian discourse.

Brew's Broadcast

The familiar chime of the Jacksonian network echoed through millions of minds, signaling the start of a new broadcast. Brew Jackson, his iridescent robes shimmering with a thousand cosmic hues, materialized on countless holographic displays across Jacksonsonville. Behind him, a stark image of Earth hung in the void, its continents crisscrossed by the scars of human activity.

"My fellow Jacksons," he began, his voice a charismatic blend of urgency and gravitas, "tonight, we grapple with a question that strikes at the very heart of our existence — a question that has challenged philosophers and scientists for millennia: What does it mean to be conscious?"

He paused, allowing the weight of the question to settle upon the collective mind of Jacksonsonville.

"We, the Jacksons, have long prided ourselves on our advanced understanding of consciousness," he continued. "Our tele-pathic unity, our harmonious relationship with our environ-ment, our commitment to ethical decision-making — these are the hallmarks of a sentient species, a species in tune with the cosmic rhythm. But what of the humans? These perplexing Earthlings, these masters of self-sabotage, these architects of their own undoing?"

He gestured toward the image of Earth, his voice rising with impassioned disbelief. "Behold a species seemingly intent on unraveling the very fabric of life! They pollute their air, plunder their resources, drive countless species to extinction, and yet they seem surprised — even outraged — by the consequences of their actions. It's as if they're caught in a loop — a cosmic feedback loop of self-inflicted suffering."

"Some argue that their behavior is simply a byproduct of primitive instincts, remnants of their evolutionary past," Brew acknowledged. "But I propose a more unsettling possibility. What if their destructive tendencies, their illogical choices, their baffling contradictions are not signs of a lack of consciousness, but rather manifestations of a profoundly flawed consciousness — a consciousness corrupted by a cosmic glitch?"

The Jacksonian network hummed with a wave of surprise and intrigue. Brew, never one to shy away from controversy, had once again disrupted their carefully constructed worldview.

"Consider their obsession with progress," he continued, "their relentless pursuit of material wealth, their insatiable hunger for more, more, more! They build empires of concrete and steel, consume resources at an unsustainable rate, and leave a trail of ecological devastation in their wake. And for what? A fleeting sense of satisfaction, a momentary rush of acquisition, a hollow victory in a game they can never truly win."

"Their behavior suggests a fundamental disconnect from the

natural order," he argued, "a disregard for the delicate balance of life, a profound misunderstanding of their place in the grand scheme of the cosmos. It's as if their programming has gone awry — their code corrupted by a cosmic virus, their essence warped by a glitch in the matrix."

He allowed his words to resonate through the collective consciousness. "This glitch manifests in their every action — from their baffling fashion choices to their self-destructive environmental practices. They seem driven by a force that is both illogical and relentless — a force that compels them to undermine their own well-being, to disrupt the harmony of their planet, to perpetuate a cycle of suffering that threatens to engulf them all."

Turning his gaze directly into the holographic eyes of his audience, Brew addressed the core of their dilemma. "And what of our dietary choices, my fellow Jacksons? If these humans are indeed the products of a cosmic glitch, what are the implications of consuming them? Are we absorbing their dysfunction, their chaos, their flawed programming? Or are we, perhaps, performing a necessary act of cosmic cleansing, purging the universe of a malignant error?"

He softened his tone, infusing his words with a plea for wisdom. "But before we leap to such drastic conclusions, let us consider our own principles — the values that define us as a species. We have always strived to act with compassion, to seek understanding before judgment, to harmonize rather than to destroy. The human enigma is not just a challenge to our intellect; it is a test of our empathy, an opportunity to evolve our understanding of consciousness and our place in the cosmos."

"Let us proceed with humility," he urged, "with curiosity, and with a deep respect for the interconnectedness of all life — even the most baffling and self-destructive. Perhaps, through continued observation and open-minded inquiry, we can uncover the root of this cosmic glitch and, in doing so, find a way to assist rather than eradicate."

As Brew concluded his broadcast, his iridescent robes settling around him like the closing of a cosmic curtain, the Jacksonian network erupted in a symphony of debate and contemplation. Brew had ignited a spark — a catalyst for introspection that would ripple through the collective consciousness of Jacksonsonville.

Brew leaned back from his console. He had shared his truth, laid bare his concerns, and now it was up to his fellow Jacksons to decide how to proceed.

Kruma approached quietly, placing a reassuring hand on his shoulder. "You did well," she said softly. "Whatever comes next, you have planted a seed. Let us hope it grows into wisdom."

Brew nodded, grateful for her unwavering support. "The path ahead is uncertain," he admitted, "but perhaps uncertainty is what we need — a moment to pause and reflect before we make decisions that could alter the course of our existence."

"Indeed," Kruma agreed. "After all, it's in the spaces between certainty that true understanding often emerges."

Harmony and Harvest

The warm, earthy aroma of roasted algae-fungi loaf filled Grag's kitchen. No shimmering culinary hologram, just a simple loaf baked to perfection. Elaborate presentations were unnecessary, Grag believed, favoring functionality. Simplicity where it served, complexity when required, this was the Jacksonian way. His four children, gathered around the table, eagerly awaited their meal.

"Papa, is it true Aunt Willa and Uncle Jack are getting two new siblings?" Quirk, the youngest, his thoughts radiating innocent curiosity, initiated the conversation.

Grag, his three-fingered hand reaching for a slice of the steaming loaf, chuckled. "Indeed, little one. They've finally convinced the incubation board that a family of five isn't quite large enough for their ambitious parenting goals."

A ripple of amusement echoed in the children's minds. Their own experiences in the incubation chambers were distant, hazy memories, a pre-conscious state of knowledge assimilation before they were awakened into their sentient selves.

Krill, the eldest, her thoughts pulsing with a contemplative green, expressed a thoughtful concern. "Five is quite a number. I remember when Quirk arrived; things got quite chaotic for a while."

Grag's wife, Ilena, whose presence emanated a comforting warmth within their telepathic circle, placed a comforting hand on Krill's shoulder. "Every new arrival brings a flurry of adjustments, my dear," she said. "But we wouldn't have it any other way, would we? A family is meant to grow, to expand its web of connections, to weave new patterns of love and experience."

"That it does," Grag agreed, glancing at his children, his heart brimming with affection. "Imagine a world where life remained stagnant, where we clung to a fixed state of being, refusing growth, denying the inherent cycle of birth and... passing."

His words, spoken casually, touched upon a deeper truth, a universal constant that even the Jacksons, with their extended lifespans, could not escape. "Dying? But why, Papa?" Quirk chimed in, a subtle note of fear underlying his question.

Grag looked at his youngest, feeling a familiar pang of melancholy. "Everything that begins must inevitably end, Quirk," he explained gently. "It is the natural order, the rhythm of the universe. Imagine if we lived eternally on this planet, Quirk. Imagine no new births, no fresh perspectives, no evolution of thought or action. Would that not become monotonous?

Wouldn't our planet turn stagnant?"

A soft ripple of sadness coursed through Quirk's thoughts, but Krill, with her innate wisdom, chimed in. "Passing is a necessary transition, Quirk, a way for life to renew itself, for new possibilities to emerge. We are but temporary guardians of consciousness, passing it on to new generations like a precious flame."

"Precisely, my dear," Grag affirmed. "The Jacksons' existence isn't defined solely by our long lifespan, but by the quality of experiences we weave into it and the knowledge we pass on to our children. Passing, while seemingly an end, is also a beginning. In dying, we release our accumulated wisdom and potential, nourishing the future."

Suddenly, Grag felt a surge in the network, an insistent tele-pathic summons. It was Leavens...

The warmth of family conversation lingered in Grag's mind as he felt the familiar tug of a telepathic summons. Leavens, his academic rival and colleague at the Jacksonian University, was reaching out with an urgency that piqued Grag's curiosity.

Excusing himself from the table, Grag stepped out into the crisp air of the neighbourhood. The option to teleport flashed briefly through his mind—a convenience most Jacksonians used without a second thought. But Grag, ever the philosopher, chose to walk.

This wasn't mere stubbornness. Among certain academic

circles, a theory had gained traction: that over-reliance on instantaneous travel could dull one's connection to the physical world. It was believed that the act of traversing space, of experiencing the journey, was crucial to maintaining a grounded perspective on reality.

As Grag's feet met the path, each step became a small act of rebellion against the easy comforts of advanced technology. The texture of the ground, the subtle shifts in temperature and air currents, the play of light across the landscape — these sensations fed into his consciousness, enriching his perception of the world around him.

His mind, now freed from the immediate concerns of family life, began to anticipate the coming debate with Leavens. Their intellectual sparring matches were legendary within the halls of the University, often pushing the boundaries of Jacksonian ethics and philosophy.

The walk allowed Grag to organize his thoughts, to feel the weight of his arguments as tangibly as the rhythmic movement of his body. By choosing this slower, more deliberate approach to travel, he was, in essence, practising the very mindfulness that underpinned much of Jacksonian philosophy.

As the spires of the Jacksonian University came into view, Grag felt a surge of intellectual excitement. The physical journey had prepared him for the mental odyssey ahead. With each step, he had not just traversed space, but had transitioned from the role of nurturing father to that of a keen academic, ready to engage in the complex dance of ideas that awaited him.

Entering the grand halls of the Academy, Grag's mind was alight with anticipation. The echo of his footsteps in the corridor seemed to herald the approaching clash of intellects. He could almost feel Leavens' impatience radiating through the telepathic link, adding more urgency to their impending encounter.

"Grag," Leavens greeted, his voice a blend of warmth and curiosity. "I must admit, your insistence on a physical meeting intrigues me. What couldn't be conveyed through our usual telepathic channels?"

Grag took a moment, weighing his words carefully. "Some discussions, Leavens, require more than just the exchange of thoughts. They demand the full spectrum of communication — the subtle shifts in expression, the nuances of tone, the shared experience of physical presence. What we're about to discuss... it's too important to risk any misunderstanding."

Leavens raised an eyebrow, his interest clearly piqued. "You speak of weighty matters, old friend. What's troubling that brilliant mind of yours?"

"It's about our ethical stance, particularly regarding humans," Grag began, his voice low and measured. "I fear we might be rushing headlong into decisions that could have far-reaching consequences. Consider this — if our current ethical position is, say, 90 out of 100, the room for improvement is minimal. But the potential for descent... that's a chasm of immeasurable depth."

Leavens' eyes narrowed, a familiar spark of intellectual challenge igniting. "Are you suggesting we halt progress for fear of missteps, Grag? Stagnation has its own perils."

"Not halt, no," Grag clarified, his gestures emphatic. "But perhaps... proceed with more caution. The universe is vast and full of unknowns. One misjudgment could send us tumbling into ethical quandaries we're ill-prepared to navigate."

Grag Jackson: "Leavens, I've been pondering our ethical accountability, especially regarding our consumption of human meatballs. While it's evident that humans' behavior appears glaringly irrational, I am convinced that we haven't explored enough. There's a need for deeper research. Our moral stance should evolve with empirical findings, shouldn't it?"

Leavens Jackson: "Indeed, Grag. However, I argue from facts and reasoning. The bridge from what 'is' to what 'ought to be' is tenuous at best. We must approach this with caution, understanding that our perceptions may be clouded by our own biases and limitations."

Grag Jackson: "Precisely, Leavens. But isn't that the crux of the issue? Our moral guidelines have long been formulated under the assumption that certain beings, like fungi, lacked complex sentience. Now, emerging evidence suggests otherwise. Shouldn't our moral compass adjust to these revelations?"

Leavens Jackson: "You make a compelling case, Grag. However, the transformation of moral principles based on new findings must be approached with a blend of caution and scientific rigor.

Our actions, driven by empathy and understanding, should not be hasty. Yet, I concede that overlooking the possible consciousness of any species might be a grave oversight on our part."

Grag Jackson: "Precisely! Our past assumptions about fungi were proven inadequate. Now, we must consider the possibility that humans, too, might possess a consciousness we've yet to fully understand. If our goal is truly to minimize suffering, then our ethical framework must be flexible enough to include any new understanding of sentience, regardless of the species."

Leavens Jackson: "It is a complex balance, Grag. While we aim to expand our moral horizons, we must also consider the practical implications of such shifts. Our societal norms, our very way of life, could be fundamentally altered. The pursuit of knowledge is crucial, but so is the stability of our society."

Grag Jackson: "Indeed, Leavens. That's why our research into human consciousness is not just academic curiosity. It's a moral imperative. We need to understand the depths of their experiences, their capacity for suffering and joy, to ensure that our actions towards them are just and ethical."

Leavens Jackson: "Your passion for this subject is commendable, Grag. But let us not forget that in our pursuit of ethical enlightenment, we must remain grounded in the realities of our world. Our decisions carry weight, not just for us, but for all the beings with whom we share this universe. We must tread this path with care, ensuring our pursuit of knowledge does not inadvertently cause harm."

Grag Jackson: "Agreed, Leavens. Our journey must be guided by both compassion and intellect. We stand at a crossroads in our society's evolution. The decisions we make now will shape our relationship with all forms of life, not just on our planet but throughout the cosmos. This is our legacy, our responsibility."

Leavens Jackson: "Your reasoning, Grag, is profound, but it dances on the edge of a perilous cliff. You speak of evolving our moral stance based on empirical findings, but where do you draw the line? If we continually adapt our morals to new evidence, do we not risk losing our foundational principles? Your concern for the fungi, while noble, may lead us down a path where we're constantly questioning and redefining our ethics, creating a society of uncertainty."

Grag Jackson: "Leavens, I see your point, but isn't that the essence of growth and progress? To adapt and evolve? Our principles shouldn't be static but dynamic, evolving as we learn more about the universe and its inhabitants. Yes, there's risk in redefining ethics, but the greater danger lies in stagnation. If we cling too tightly to outdated views, we risk becoming obsolete in our own society."

Leavens Jackson: "But Grag, there's comfort in stability, in knowing the boundaries and rules. Continual change breeds chaos. We must balance our thirst for knowledge and ethical evolution with the need for a stable society. Not every new piece of evidence should upend our way of life. It's about discernment, about knowing when to adapt and when to hold firm."

Grag Jackson: "True, Leavens, discernment is key. But

shouldn't our ultimate goal be to minimize suffering and maximize well-being for all beings."

Leavens Jackson interrupted: "Grag! you must understand this—Earth is a place full of life. Our Jackson Council has long debated the ethics of interacting with its inhabitants. We have a solemn agreement not to substantially interfere with the affairs of this world, but rather to observe and learn.

"You, Grag, see humans as beings of potential, worthy of our closer involvement. I appreciate your perspective, but our existing knowledge derived from research and observations has led me to a different conclusion. Yes, there are beings on this planet, like the orcas and elephants, who have shown remarkable signs of sentience. They live in harmony with their environment, displaying a level of intelligence and emotional depth that compels our respect and non-interference.

"However, when it comes to humans, the situation is complex. Humans often exhibit a perplexing disregard for their own environment and other species. This contradiction in their behavior makes them unique among Earth's inhabitants.

"For me, the most glaring example of human irrationality lies in their treatment of the forests. They seem to be the sole species on Earth intent on eradicating the diversity of trees, replacing vast and thriving ecosystems with singular planta-tions. This destruction wreaks havoc on biodiversity, and the cycle perpetuates itself, growing ever more destructive. They replace life-filled landscapes with cold, concrete structures, emit gases that contribute to planetary warming, all while attempting to counteract the rising temperatures with warm clothing. Their behaviour appears to be irrational from an environmental standpoint and from the individual human point of view. It's a paradoxical conundrum of self-inflicted harm!

"Consider the numbers: an estimated 12 billion humans roam Earth, whereas only around two million orcas, 500 thousand elephants, and one million bears coexist. Yet, humans consistently engage in activities that undermine the well-being of their own planet. It appears they possess a unique talent for sabotaging their own habitat. It looks like they multiply as pests on the planet, and according to our monitoring data, the more humans that appear, the worse the condition of life on that planet becomes.

"The evidence, from our vantage point, suggests that humans are, for the most part, irrational beings. While I acknowledge the inherent uncertainty in our knowledge, their meatballs, from our current understanding, appear to be the most logical alternative. A deeper look into their society would demand that we interfere with Earth's environment more drastically, and our current observations indicate this to be unnecessary disturbance to the lives of the sentient beings of Earth.

"Our current reliance on fungi, as we've recently discovered, may not be as harmless as we once thought. The ethical implications of consuming a sentient organism have led us to reconsider our food sources. In this context, humans, with their seemingly lesser impact on the cosmic balance, appear as a viable alternative.

Our primary goal remains to find a sustainable, ethical solution that aligns with our principles, and for now, humans seem to fit this criterion."

With a wink, Leavens concluded his monologue, leaving Grag to ponder the cosmic absurdity of Earth and its quirky inhabitants.

Grag politely conceded to Leavens' arguments, but deep inside he was uncomfortable with the idea but felt like he could not counter Leaven's point. So they went on about their own business.

8

Gunnar and Grag Make a Plan

Amidst the ongoing discussions about human meatballs, chaos had emerged from Brew's broadcast, leading the Jacksons to grow suspicious. The notion that humans exhibiting such irrational behavior patterns was potentially indicative of an AI glitch sparked a curious turn of events. Grag thought the project, centered around human meatballs, was progressing too hastily, potentially overlooking the grave injustice of causing immense suffering to individual beings.

Curiously, Brew's perception of human irrationality aligned with what Grag sought — caution. One might expect Grag to feel relieved, but that's not the Jacksons' way. They don't fixate on outcomes unless philosophically aligned with their perceptions. They strive for utmost precision in their views; it's just their way.

Bewildered by these events, Grag consulted his friend Gunnar Jackson, a highly regarded student of conscious operations at

Jackson University. Entering Gunnar's room, Grag found him sitting, using his telepathic telescope.

Grag shared his concerns about the human meatball initiative. Withdrawing human meatballs from consumption for health reasons was a measure of caution. The rationale was that ingesting such irrational beings that could only be a result of a glitch in AI programming might be detrimental to the Jacksons' health in the long-term. But Grag wanted the human meatball project to be more cautiously conducted not due to possible long-term consequences but for ethical considerations.

"I consider this too speculative," Grag expressed. "From our perspective, human life appears irrational, but it's presumptuous to assume they lack consciousness. How can we easily conclude whether or not they are the result of AI?"

Gunnar, intrigued by Grag's inquiry, opened a bottle of the Jacksons' typical buzzy beverage, serving them both. "Grag, you're overly concerned about consciousness, but this question is more irrelevant than it appears. This is more a matter of social perception than a hard fact of reality. It depends on the angle from which we infer consciousness. From one viewpoint, one might argue that we, the Jacksons, are not conscious beings, as we embody only consciousness."

He continued, "Consciousness is often shrouded in mystery, perceived as ethereal, beyond the grasp of science. But what are we? Fundamentally, a collection of about a hundred trillion cells, each functioning like a tiny robot. None possess individual awareness, ponder existential questions, or admire sunsets.

How can this be?

"In this view, beings we recognize as conscious, like us, the gorpods, and orcas, are coherent groupings that integrate the basic consciousness pervasive in the universe. This integration, achieved through complex physical processes, suggests that at the most fundamental level, everything boils down to physical interactions. These interactions occur in humans too, explaining the behavior we deem irrational."

Grag pondered, "Well, Gunnar, doesn't this corroborate my viewpoint? As they are all consequences of physical processes, much like we are, shouldn't we be empathetic towards consuming them?"

Gunnar countered, "No, this goes directly against what I said. This just shows you that whether one is conscious or not is a matter of perspective. It's possible to construct a narrative where everything is conscious, and at the same time, it's possible for nothing to be conscious, just a mere consequence of the various possibilities of matter grouping itself. What I mean is, this is much more of a social question. We, the Jacksons, have values of preserving nature and life, and our comfort as intricate beings. This is the Jacksons' view of consciousness: a being that goes about its intentions while preserving its means for increasing its survivability."

"Also, eating our fungi is uncomfortable for most Jacksons, and we will struggle to find a food source without committing any injustices. That is the nature of things. So, as the demand to find a substitute for fungi is dire, we must look for an alternative.

72

These humans in our cosmic vicinity appear to be a disgrace to the environment. So, from my perspective, they seem a good alternative with smaller risks of injustice."

Grag, with a demeanor reminiscent of a concerned insisted "The individual experience, Gunnar! That's what matters. Conscious or not, rational or otherwise, if a being can experience suffering—and suffer intricately at that—it's simply unfair for us, the Jacksons, to be the cause of such misery. Our actions must be guided by the respect for this suffering mechanism."

Gunnar, stroking his chin thoughtfully, responded with a mix of resignation and pragmatic realism, "Grag, my friend, this is an unavoidable truth of our existence. It's unfortunate, yes, but inescapable. We've not yet discovered a method of sustenance that guarantees zero suffering. Nature, in its ruthless efficiency, designed a system where survival often necessitates preying upon others. Even if they suffer, it isn't sufficient reason to alter our course."

Grag, not one to relent easily, countered, "Then, Gunnar, we must delve deeper. We must study the individual human senses, their impact on the environment, their capabilities. Only through understanding can we make the fairest assessment possible. We owe them that much."

Gunnar, with a nod, acknowledged, "Studying is never an issue. We are, after all, dedicated to learning. But we must craft a plan that does not violate the Non-Interference Agreement with Earth. This, Grag, will be our greatest challenge."

They continued by ushering a proposition to the Krooks Jackson International Committee. This proposal outlined the necessity for deeper studies on humans to formulate a better assessment of appropriate actions. For understanding human inner sensations, they suggested the abduction of two individual humans. The first, a middle-aged, healthy individual who wore clothing inappropriate for their environment, specifically one of those who wore suits and kept walking around in 35-degree Celsius plus temperatures. The second would be an individual who tended to dress more adequately for their environment.

They aimed to compare the two beings' synapses and internal functioning. This was to determine if some humans still possessed rationality, and if so, perhaps some had been plagued with a type of counterproductive disease, which would explain a lot. The objective of this study was to conclude whether their inner function caused them to suffer, and what it was like to experience this. The question could not be perfectly answered, as one might never be able to experience the world as the other perfectly. However, they aimed to attain a good model of what their experience was like.

In terms of the suffering caused to the abducted humans, they intended to sedate them and communicate placidly through telepathy about their goals before sending them back to Earth. They would teleport themselves to a spaceship that would orbit Earth's moon, thus not taking the humans too far and avoiding unpredictable damages. They planned to conduct the tests within three hours, which should be sufficient to avoid significant harm to the individual subjects, and then send them back to Earth.

If things went awry, they would give up on the mission, send the humans back, and return with a report. The idea was to gain their agreement, engage in communication, and assess them through the x-ray telepathic machine built on their stellar system's moon closest to Jacksonsonville. With the x-ray results, they would have a better assessment of what ingesting human meatballs would do to the Jacksons' health.

In this mission, stage two involved a plan to make contact with the orcas to access their view of humans. They would ask why there were so many of them, and what their views were on human actions, to have a fairer assessment of how human behavior stood in relation to the Jacksons' moral perception. They believed this study would provide them with much-needed information for the current conundrum.

In the meticulous plan crafted by the Jacksons for their 'orca stage', their approach and contact with the orcas was designed to be as non-intrusive as possible. Using their spaceship, they would cautiously enter the orcas' natural habitat, maintaining a respectful distance to minimize environmental disruption. This initial contact was critical in establishing a foundation of trust and communicating their peaceful intentions to the orcas.

Throughout their interactions, the Jacksons were committed to upholding the highest ethical standards. They recognized the importance of respecting the orcas' autonomy and would seek their consent before proceeding with any form of communication. This approach ensured that the orcas would not feel threatened or coerced, acknowledging that the opportunity to communicate with another intelligent species was a privilege rather than a right.

Following this study, the plan was to engage in a thorough debriefing process, integrating the insights gained into their broader ethical framework, considering the orca's perspective together with their findings from direct human test results, and broadcasting their findings in the all-pervasive social media, so that together the Jacksons could think on the more appropriate course of action.

Grag and Gunnar, having formulated a detailed research proposal, recognized the strategic importance of involving Marvin Jackson in their project. Marvin, a renowned nutritionist on Jacksonsonville, had been a prominent advocate for the health benefits of consuming human meatballs. His involvement, they believed, was crucial for the success of their endeavor.

Their decision to approach Marvin was driven by two key factors. First, there was a natural alignment of scientific interests. Marvin's research had primarily focused on the nutritional benefits of human meatballs. Grag and Gunnar's project, aimed at exploring deeper health implications, particularly the long-term effects on Jacksonian physiology, would potentially open new avenues in Marvin's research. They anticipated that the prospect of unearthing new scientific data about a subject he was already invested in would appeal to Marvin's scholarly curiosity.

Second, they considered Marvin's influence and standing within the Jacksonian community. His endorsement of their project would lend it the credibility and visibility it needed. Grag and Gunnar understood that having Marvin, a respected figure, on their side could significantly sway public and academic opinion. This was particularly crucial given the skepticism of the Krooks Committee, a body known for its conservative stance on research funding and approval. Marvin's support could be a catalyst in transforming their research from a speculative endeavor into a legitimate scientific inquiry.

With this in mind, Grag and Gunnar prepared to approach Marvin. They planned to highlight how their collaborative research could mutually benefit their scientific pursuits, hoping to pique his interest and secure his support for their ambitious project.

Marvin Jackson, the most respected nutritionist in Jackson-sonville, was the head of the entire Department of Nutritional Studies and had been the mastermind behind orchestrating the whole fungi-based diet followed by the majority on their planet. Before Marvin's revolutionary idea, the Jacksons were suffering from an infectious disease crisis, primarily caused by the fungi growing within Jacksonsonville. They used to get their resources from these fungi and by eating small rodent-like creatures called Mirpods, which lived a subterranean lifestyle. The fungi, some edible and others extremely toxic, were the main cause of infectious diseases. They invaded the Jacksons' metabolic systems in various ways, entrenching themselves in water sources and food.

Marvin's idea to extract all the fungi and transfer them to an orbiting space station was incredible and revolutionary. It re-moved the infectious fungi from their planet and created spaces where edible fungi could be monitored and tailored according to the Jacksons' and other beings' needs on Jacksonsonville. This space station, which the Jacksons called Fungihsonsville, allowed the edible fungi to thrive in a controlled environment, free from the hazards they posed on the planet.

Marvin planned the creation of multiple fungi species specifically tailored for the Jacksons' metabolic systems in this space station just outside Jacksonsonville. There, they let the fungi live out their lifecycle, consuming the whole system of the space station themselves. By extracting the fungi and bacteria from the planet, they eradicated the plague of infectious diseases affecting the Jacksons and other inhabitants of Jacksonville.

However, Marvin noticed that, as consequence of sticking to a fungi-based diet, since they had started the fungi program, the physical capabilities of the Jacksons were decreasing. They maintained their cognitive abilities but were getting smaller and physically weaker. The average size of a Jackson used to be around 1.13 meters, weighing about 42 kg. Since the program's inception, the average weight of the Jacksons had decreased by 1.2 percent, which wasn't much but had Marvin interested in finding even better and more sustainable sources.

With ethicists like Quaint Jackson promoting the idea of fungi suffering, and after showing the thriving environment the space station created for the fungi, there was a growing need to promote a less exploitative way of dealing with fungi. Earth had become prominent on Marvin's radar, as all sorts of radio frequencies were being sent from there into space. Marvin noted that humans existed there in crazy numbers, so he thought that only 1,000 humans per month would provide a significant alternative for the Jackson diet and would signify little impact on their society.

He started modeling through a long telescopic x-ray the human anatomy and how it would work in the Jackson digestive system. From his yet anecdotal modeling results, it seemed that it would transpire quite well, so he started advocating for experimental tests of human meatball eating, which resulted in the whole sets of discussions being taken there.

****

Marvin Jackson sat in his office, deeply engrossed in reading the research proposal sent by Grag and Gunnar. As he flipped through the pages, he couldn't help but be impressed by the creativity and depth of their ideas. The proposal outlined a plan to study the physiology and consciousness of humans, a species that had recently become the center of a controversial dietary trend on Jacksonsonville.

The proposal came at a time when peculiar cults and theories were circulating among the Jacksons, with some believing that humans were merely creations of an Artificial Intelligence. Marvin, always the skeptic, found these theories far-fetched. He had always viewed humans as basic-level individuals whose counterproductive lifestyle and rampant reproduction were merely consequences of their irrationality. The idea of humans being AI creations seemed to him an overly complicated explanation for a simpler reality.

What truly fascinated Marvin about Grag and Gunnar's proposal was the opportunity to delve into the physiology of a human. The prospect of studying an entirely different species, understanding their biological systems, and assessing their potential nutritional value for the Jacksons was an exciting new challenge for him. He saw immense potential in this research, not just for academic curiosity but for its practical implications in enhancing the Jacksonian diet.

Marvin was already formulating strategies for the project, envisioning ways to incorporate human-based nutrition into the Jacksons' dietary regime. He believed that if done ethically and sustainably, this could be a significant addition to their food sources, possibly addressing the physical decline they had observed since the adoption of the fungi diet.

With a sense of determination and intrigue, Marvin signed off on the proposal. He was ready to collaborate with Grag and Gunnar, bringing his expertise and resources to this groundbreaking study. In his mind, he began planning the logistics, from the safe and ethical acquisition of human subjects to the detailed analysis of their biological makeup.

Emboldened by this development, Grag and Gunnar proceeded to finalize their proposal for submission to the Krooks Committee. They incorporated Marvin's insights and suggestions, ensuring the proposal was comprehensive and addressed any possible reservations the committee might have. The document now outlined not only the scientific and ethical framework of their study but also highlighted the potential benefits of their findings for the broader Jacksonian society.

9

Testing the Humans

The two human subjects, Taylor Swift and Arthur Neves, lay unconscious within the sterile confines of the spaceship laboratory. The Jacksons, buzzing with a mixture of scientific curiosity and philosophical apprehension, prepared to delve into the depths of human consciousness.

Grag, ever the advocate for ethical considerations, initiated the testing process with a sense of trepidation. He carefully monitored the vitals of the subjects, ensuring their comfort and safety throughout the experiment. Marvin, focused on the nutritional aspects, meticulously documented every physiological response, eager to unravel the mysteries of human biology. Gunnar, the resident philosopher, observed with a keen eye, ready to dissect the humans' reactions and weave them into the tapestry of Jacksonian understanding.

Their first experiment involved exposing the humans to a variety of stimuli, ranging from soothing sounds and calming scents to jarring noises and unpleasant odors. The Jacksons observed the subtle shifts in brain activity, heart rate, and muscle tension, meticulously recording each response.

"Fascinating," Marvin remarked, studying the data. "Their reactions to sensory stimuli appear quite similar to our own. The heightened response to unpleasant stimuli suggests a survival mechanism designed to avoid danger, much like our aversion to the toxic fungi back on Jacksonsonville."

"Indeed," Gunnar pondered, stroking his chin thoughtfully. "However, there seems to be an additional layer of complexity in their reactions. Observe how the subject identified as 'Taylor Swift' exhibits a heightened response to the image of a large feline creature. Perhaps this indicates a deep-seated fear or aversion ingrained in their species."

Grag, ever cautious, interjected, "We must be careful not to jump to conclusions. Their reactions could be influenced by individual experiences or cultural factors we are not yet aware of."

The next stage of the experiment involved altering the humans' clothing. The Jacksons, accustomed to their simple, functional attire, were intrigued by the wide array of fabrics, textures, and styles worn by humans. They carefully removed the subjects' clothing, replacing them with a variety of garments ranging from loose, comfortable robes to tight, restrictive outfits.

The humans' reactions to this change were perplexing to the Jacksons. Both subjects exhibited signs of discomfort and anxiety when fully naked, their heart rates increasing and their muscles tensing.

"This is most peculiar," Grag remarked, observing the data. "Why would they experience such discomfort when unclothed? It seems illogical from a purely practical standpoint."

Marvin, ever the pragmatist, offered a theory. "Perhaps it is a matter of temperature regulation. Their bodies appear less adept at adapting to temperature changes than ours. The lack of clothing may cause them to feel vulnerable to the elements."

Gunnar, however, had a different perspective. "I believe there is a deeper, philosophical explanation. Observe how they attempt to cover themselves even when the temperature is controlled. This suggests a sense of shame or modesty, a concept that appears absent in our society."

"Shame?" Grag echoed, perplexed. "But what could they possibly be ashamed of? Their bodies are merely biological vessels, no different from our own."

Gunnar continued to muse, "Perhaps this aversion to nakedness is a societal construct, a learned behavior ingrained so deeply within their culture that it has become a fundamental part of their identity. It could be that they associate nakedness with vulnerability or a loss of social status, reflecting complex layers of human consciousness."

As the Jacksons absorbed Gunnar's analysis, they felt compelled to explore further. They initiated a deeper telepathic investigation into the humans' thought processes, shifting from mere physical observation to probing the psychological underpinnings of human discomfort with nudity. This phase of the experiment moved beyond the tangible reactions to explore the intangible feelings of shame and modesty.

Despite their sophisticated methods, the Jacksons found themselves confounded by the irrational nature of human shame—there seemed to be no logical foundation for the intense discomfort associated with nakedness. This emotional response appeared to be an arbitrary construct, entirely shaped by cultural influences rather than any biological necessity.

Marvin adjusted his robe, a hint of excitement coloring his typically reserved demeanor. "After thoroughly analyzing their responses and delving into their thought processes," he began, his voice measured yet imbued with a sense of discovery, "it appears increasingly plausible that the hypothesis suggesting artificial creation of humans might hold water. Their physiological and psychological reactions, particularly their uniform response to shame associated with nudity, do not align with any natural evolutionary advantages or survival mechanisms we can discern."

He continued, articulating each word with clinical precision, "This uniformity of response, seen across such distinct individuals as Taylor Swift and Arthur Neves, hints at something profound. It suggests that this sense of shame, rather than arising naturally, may have been artificially embedded within them. The absence of a clear, rational explanation for this behavior in our telepathic explorations leaves us with a compelling scenario:

84

these characteristics might have been designed, implanted into their psyche as a part of their creation."

Marvin paused, allowing the implications of his statement to permeate the room. "If we consider this from a broader perspective," he added, "it seems that this artificially induced shame could serve to regulate social behaviors and maintain order, a tool embedded not by evolution but by design. This uniformity in their emotional responses, especially in scenarios devoid of any practical threat, reinforces the hypothesis that humans may have been engineered with these specific traits as a means of cultural or even bio-engineered control."

His report concluded with a thoughtful nod, suggesting a shift in the Jacksons' approach to their study — perhaps what they needed to explore next was not just what made humans human, but who, if anyone, had a hand in their making.

The Jacksons, faced with this complexity, decided to expand their study to include a broader sample of humans to further explore the variability in societal impact and the potential engineered enhancement of certain individuals. This phase aimed to discern whether these traits were indeed artificially implanted and how they influenced human social dynamics on a larger scale.

Three days into the extended phase of their experiment, the Jacksons escalated their research by temporarily removing thirteen humans from various global locations, analyzing them across multiple dimensions: physical, biological, and psychological. The findings remained consistent with the initial subjects in terms of physiological and cognitive diversity, affirming a standard range of human variability.

However, the social impact of these removals varied dramatically. While some individuals' absences went nearly unnoticed, others, like Taylor Swift, incited massive upheavals. The scale of searches and public reaction varied wildly; in the case of Swift, the response was extreme to the point of tragedy, with some individuals reportedly taking their own lives out of despair over her disappearance.

This alarming outcome sparked a critical discussion among the Jacksons, particularly between Gunnar and Grag, about the ethical implications of their experiment.

Gunnar, visibly disturbed by the human reactions, suggested, "We must consider halting the program. The data we've gathered shows a pattern of extreme and irrational behavior that our intervention seems to exacerbate. Taylor Swift's absence alone has triggered a disproportionate response, indicating that our actions are meddling with deeply ingrained social and psychological constructs."

Grag, always the ethical compass of the group, agreed, "This experiment was intended to uncover information about human nature, not to cause harm. The unforeseen consequences we're witnessing suggest that our interference, even if temporary, is too invasive. It's becoming clear that our presence and actions are activating some sort of latent trigger in the human behavioral software."

The Jacksons convened to review their findings and the unexpected social chaos their experiment had caused. The discussion led to a consensus that while the data supported the hypothesis of possible artificial enhancement or creation of humans—given the irrational and varied responses to their manipulations—the ethical cost was too high.

With heavy hearts, they decided to terminate the experiment and return to Jacksonsonville. The mission had provided them with profound insights into human social structures and individual significance, but at a higher social cost than anticipated. It was concluded that the Jacksons' interference, though scholarly in intent, had acted as a catalyst for extreme behaviors rooted in the complex web of human emotional and societal frameworks.

Upon their return, they planned to present their findings to the broader Jacksonian community. The data would be used to assess whether their theories on artificial human creation held merit and to decide how, if at all, they should engage with humanity moving forward. The overwhelming reaction to their tests suggested a complex interplay between human societal constructs and individual importance, potentially manipulated by design—a concept that would undoubtedly spark fierce debates among the Jacksonians about the ethics of further interference and the moral responsibilities of their advanced observational capabilities.

****

Regarding stage 2 of the project, as the groundwork for the

human study was being laid, another crucial component of Grag and Gunnar's project was set into motion: the orca contact mission. This part of the plan, vital for understanding the broader ecological and ethical implications of their research, was to be led by Glugi Jackson, a newcomer to the project with a strong interest in interspecies communication.

Glugi, known for his enthusiasm for making contact with other intelligent species, had volunteered to lead the mission. His approach was to engage the orcas in a direct dialogue, using the Jacksons' advanced telepathic technologies to communicate and gather insights without causing disruption or harm to the orca communities.

Interview with Maximine: Understanding the Orca Perspective

Glugi's interaction with Maximine, a prominent orca leader, was structured as an open-ended interview, allowing for a free-flowing exchange of ideas and perspectives. The format was designed to be respectful and non-intrusive, acknowledging the orcas' intelligence and autonomy.

During the interview, Maximine shared insights that were both enlightening and disturbing, painting a picture of how orcas perceived human activities and their impacts on the marine environment. The orcas' observations highlighted a range of human behaviors that seemed bizarre and often harmful from an ecological standpoint.

Key Points from the Interview:

1. Artistic Misunderstandings: Maximine discussed how humans attempted to teach a dolphin to paint, interpreting artistic ability as a sign of intelligence. This was puzzling to the orcas, who considered their own art forms, like bubble patterns and synchronized swimming, as natural expressions of their culture, not requiring artificial mediums like canvas.

2. Communication Barriers: The practice of throwing plastic bottles with messages into the sea was seen as a counterproductive and polluting form of communication by the orcas. This human behavior conflicted with the orcas' more holistic view of communication, which emphasizes clarity and respect for the environment.

3. The Concept of Selfies and Whale Watching: The orcas were perplexed by humans' obsession with capturing images of themselves with marine life, risking safety for a photograph. This behavior was contrasted with the orcas' approach to memorable experiences, which they valued for their intrinsic, not documented, worth.

4. Environmental Impact of Human Celebrations: Maximine expressed concern over activities like fireworks, which caused widespread panic among marine life. These human celebrations were seen as destructive rituals that disregarded the well-being of other species.

Reflections and Implications for the Jacksons:

The insights provided by Maximine and other orcas during the interview would play a crucial role in shaping the ethical framework of the Jacksons' research and their future interactions with Earth. The stark differences in perspective emphasized the need for a cautious and respectful approach to studying and potentially integrating humans into their diet.

Glugi's report, enriched with these firsthand accounts from the orcas, added a critical dimension to the ongoing debate about the moral implications of consuming human meatballs. It highlighted the complexity of interspecies relationships and the importance of considering the broader ecological consequences of the Jacksons' dietary choices.

As the project moved forward, the insights from the orca interview would be integrated with the findings from the human study, helping the Jacksons make informed decisions that aligned with their values of preserving life and minimizing suffering across species. This holistic approach underscored the Jacksons' commitment to ethical science and their respect for all intelligent life forms, setting a standard for future endeavors in their interstellar explorations.

Grag's Report on the Human Experimentation Mission:

To the Esteemed Krooks Committee,

  I present a conclusive analysis of our recent mission to study human physiology, psychology, and societal structures, incorporating insights from both the direct human experimentation and the orca contact mission. Our primary objective was to assess the suitability of humans as a potential food source for the Jacksons, while also considering the broader ecological and ethical implications of such a decision.

Our initial hypothesis, based on long-distance observations, suggested that humans were a simple, possibly irrational species with a counterproductive lifestyle and uncontrolled reproductive tendencies. This hypothesis was primarily informed by their detrimental impact on their environment and the seemingly chaotic nature of their societies. However, direct interaction with human subjects "Taylor Swift" and "Arthur Neves" revealed a far more complex and perplexing reality.

While their physiological responses to stimuli were remarkably similar to our own, their psychological makeup presented intriguing anomalies. The most striking example was their profound discomfort and sense of shame associated with nakedness, a concept entirely foreign to Jacksonian culture. This aversion to nudity, despite the absence of any logical basis from a survival or evolutionary standpoint, led us to delve deeper into the human psyche through telepathic investigation.

We discovered a complex web of emotions, memories, and societal conditioning that influenced their behavior. The uniformity of the shame response across diverse individuals suggests the possibility of intentional design or manipulation, as if this emotional response was artificially embedded within them. Further analysis of human clothing practices reinforced this notion, with garments appearing to serve as external control mechanisms, reinforcing societal constructs and behavioral patterns.

The subsequent phase of our experiment, involving the temporary removal of additional human subjects, revealed a disparity in societal impact. While some individuals' absences went unnoticed, others, like Taylor Swift, triggered massive social upheavals and widespread distress. This suggests a hierarchy of importance or influence within the human population, potentially indicative of deliberate design or selective enhancement.

Parallel to the human study, the orca contact mission, led by Glugi Jackson, provided invaluable insights into the ecological impact of human activities. The orcas' observations highlighted a range of human behaviors that seemed bizarre and often harmful from an ecological standpoint. Their perspectives on artistic expression, communication, and interactions with marine life starkly contrasted with our own, emphasizing the need for a cautious and respectful approach when considering humans as a potential food source.

The integration of findings from both missions paints a picture of a species that is a complex interplay of natural and artificial forces. Humans exhibit behaviors and societal structures that suggest potential manipulation by design, yet their reactions to our interventions were unpredictable and often extreme.

The reported suicides following Taylor Swift's disappearance were particularly concerning, leading us to hypothesize that the removal of certain individuals triggers a "bug" within the human "software", resulting in chaotic and inconsistent societal responses. This lack of predictable reaction patterns raised significant ethical concerns and prompted the unanimous decision to halt the mission in accordance with the precautionary principle.

Despite the termination of the experiment, we believe that the mission has collected sufficient data to spark significant debate within the Krooks Committee and guide future decisions regarding our interactions with humans. The evidence gathered suggests that humans, while potentially suitable as a food source, present a complex ethical dilemma due to their unpredictable nature and the potential for unforeseen consequences resulting from our interference.

We recommend a thorough analysis of the collected data, considering both the initial hypothesis and the groundwork insights, to determine the most appropriate course of action moving forward.

While the human experiment has presented us with significant ethical challenges, it has also provided invaluable insights into the nature of consciousness, artificial intelligence, and the complex interplay between natural and artificial forces in the universe.

Respectfully submitted,

Grag Jackson

Head of the human research groundwork mission

Jacksonsonville

10

The Robes of Judgment

To the Esteemed Members of the Krooks Committee,

I hope this letter finds you in robust health and with the wisdom required to navigate the complexities of our current predicament. It is with a heavy but hopeful heart that I submit for your consideration and subsequent plebiscite the Human Harvest Programme, a meticulously crafted initiative designed to address the dire nutritional needs of our populace while rigorously upholding the highest standards of ethical conduct in our interactions with the human species.

Understanding the gravity of the decision before us, it is essential to articulate the operational aspects of the proposed programme and the moral rationale that underpins each phase of its implementation. In the spirit of transparency and ethical rigor, the following details are intended to provide a comprehensive overview of the programme's structure, emphasizing our commitment to the principles of ethical treatment and minimal impact.

The programme begins with the Acquisition phase, where,

through the use of our advanced teleportation technology, selected individuals will be transported from Earth to our facilities on Jacksonsonville. This technology ensures that the process is imperceptible, minimizing psychological distress for both the individuals involved and their communities. The selection criteria for these individuals are strictly based on minimizing societal disruption and are informed by an extensive analysis of demographic data to ensure that only those whose absence will be least noticed are chosen. This approach not only reduces the impact on human societies but also aligns with our ethical commitment to cause the least harm.

In this initial phase, the number of individuals selected for transport will be capped at 2.5 million, representing a very small percentage of the Earth's population. This specific number has been calculated to ensure that there will be no need for further extractions, thus preventing unnecessary disturbance to Earth's societal and environmental balance. Importantly, this amount ensures that there will be enough genetic variety within the samples, with a composition of approximately 70 percent females. This ratio is designed to extend the chance for individuals to freely choose partners for mating, thereby supporting the psychological well-being and social stability of the harvested population.

The mating period will be organized to occur once every Jacksonville star rotation, aligning with the natural reproductive cycles and social rituals of the human species. This periodic approach to mating is intended to provide a sense of normalcy and continuity for the individuals involved, reflecting our commitment to maintaining an environment that respects their inherent social and biological rhythms.

It is important to acknowledge, however, that despite our rigorous selection process and the advanced technology employed, there *may be unforeseen consequences where the extraction of certain individuals could inadvertently cause disproportionate confusion and distress within human society. This is a possibility we must consider, especially given previous findings in our groundwork studies that suggest an error in the coding behavior of humans that could trigger such extreme reactions. A notable instance observed was with the individual known as Taylor Swift, whose removal led to significantly heightened emotional responses and social unrest, far exceeding our initial projections.*

Upon arrival, these individuals will be introduced to our Assimilation Facilities, meticulously designed to provide comfort and a semblance of Earth's environment. The diet provided will replicate what humans typically consume, based on our research findings which indicate that humans thrive on a diet that includes ground worms, commonly known as earthlings, along with roots and typical vegetables from Earth, as well as insects. All these components will be sustainably harvested on our moon, in a large chamber specifically adapted to support humans and their dietary needs. This controlled environment will ensure a continuous and consistent supply of food, requiring only initial samples from Earth to begin cultivation.

The next phase involves what we must acknowledge as the most sensitive aspect of the programme — the Ethical Termination process. Here, our methods embody the commitment to ensure that the end of life is conducted with the utmost respect and minimal suffering. Utilizing a method that induces a deep, peaceful unconsciousness followed by a painless cessation of life functions, we adhere to our moral obligations. Each step of this process will be overseen by a board of ethical reviewers, including both Jacksonian ethicists.

Post-termination, the programme stipulates a comprehensive Utilization Protocol, where every part of the biological material obtained is used efficiently and respectfully. This phase honours the sacrifice and ensures that no part of this sacrifice goes to waste. Innovations in biotechnology allow us to convert biological materials into a variety of beneficial products, ranging from nutritional supplements to pharmaceutical compounds, thus maximizing the utility of the harvested materials and contributing significantly to the health and well-being of our populace.

To ensure that the Human Harvest Programme operates within the strictest ethical guidelines, the entire process from acquisition to utilization will be transparent and subject to continuous oversight. An Ethical Oversight Board, as previously mentioned, will conduct regular reviews and make their findings available to the Jacksonian public.

In closing, I urge the Krooks Committee to consider the broader implications of this project. As Jacksonians, we have always prided ourselves on our ability to lead with compassion and foresight. This programme is built upon a foundation of ethical consideration that sets a precedent for how advanced civilizations ought to resolve complex survival challenges.

Thank you for your consideration of this vital matter. I look forward to your decision and am at your disposal to provide any further information or clarification you might require.

Respectfully,
Marvin Jackson

The grand hall of the Jacksons' Academy buzzed with a palpable tension as the members of the Krooks Committee gathered for a momentous occasion. The air crackled with anticipation, the weight of the impending decision hanging heavy over the assembly. Krooks Jackson, the esteemed chair of the committee, stood at the podium, his multifaceted eyes surveying the diverse gathering of Jacksons.

"Ladies, gentlemen, and everyone in between, it is I, Krooks Jackson, your humble chair at this council of kinship and calamity. Tonight, we are gathered to ponder the threads of fate and fortune that have bound us together — whether for better or worse.

As I stand before you, presiding over this motley assembly with the gavel of both privilege and burden, I find myself oscillating between amusement and despair, nostalgia and contempt. Yes, contempt, for how can one not recoil at the absurd theatrics of greed masquerading as grief? It is a spectacle, where each of you, my dear Jacksonians, play your part with a gusto that would surely earn a nod from the bard.

But let us not kid ourselves with undue romanticism. We are not here to outdo each other in eloquence or empathy. No, this is a far baser script we enact, one of division and dissension, where the stakes are the very soul of the human lineage, if there may lie a soul in any sense you might consider.

Consider, if you will, the ludicrousness of our plight. Here we are, bickering over trinkets and titles while outside these gilded walls, the world spins on, blissfully indifferent to our 'tragedy'. And yet, within these confines, every gesture, every word weighs heavy with history and consequence.

Some of you, with furrowed brows and sharp tongues, have already laid bare your grievances, painting vivid pictures of past slights and oversights. Others have sat in silent judgment, your eyes darting like daggers, your minds calculating the cost of alliance and opposition. And amidst this chaos, I—your humble chair jacksonian—must navigate the storm, steering us toward some semblance of resolution.

It would be easy, oh so easy, to let you tear each other apart, to watch as you dismantle yourselves in the endlessness of pondering. But that would be a failure of my duty, a betrayal of the role I have been given. Therefore, I propose a different course, one that might yet salvage both our fortunes and our faces.

Let us call for a plebiscite, a direct voice from each of you, not filtered through legalese or swayed by silver-tongued persuasion. Let there be a vote, clear and unequivocal, on the path we shall take as a family. Shall we divide the estate equally among all stakeholders, ensuring that no one is left wanting? Or shall we adhere strictly to the dictates of the will, with all its precise allocations and implicit hierarchies?

The choice is yours to make, and make it you must, for I refuse to dictate terms to those who must live with the consequences. Reflect, then, on what you truly seek from this gathering. Is it wealth? Is it justice? Or is it perhaps something as simple yet elusive as inner peace?

As you ponder these questions, I ask you to consider the legacy we wish to leave for those Jacksons who will come after us. Will they speak of the Jacksons as a family torn apart by greed, or will they tell tales of a clan that rose above the plight of self-doubt to forge a new path of unity and respect?

To the outside observer, we might appear as mere squabblers over a substantial estate, a family caught in avarice and discord. But ah, there is so much more beneath the surface, layers of complexity that define and, dare I say, dignify our saga.

As I muse upon our lineage, it strikes me that we Jacksons are creatures of immense passion and profound contradiction. We have always valued the robes we wear, the symbolism stitched into every thread—empathy, morals, respect. These robes, they are armours—armours that shield our vulnerabilities and guide our ambitions.

Take, for instance, our dear cousin Grag, whose efforts to seek consciousness in realms where others see mere void are both admirable and, to some, absurd. Grag sees beyond the tangible, quests for meaning in the ethereal, the unknown. His beliefs, while often dismissed as the ramblings of a fervent dreamer, are not without merit. They remind us that there is more to this existence than the eye can see, more to life than the cold hard assets we now divide amongst ourselves.

And yet, while I commend Greg's boundless spirit, I must also acknowledge the practicalities that govern our world. His pursuit, noble as it may be, is a luxury, a flight of fancy that our current predicament can barely afford. There is truth, perhaps, in his wild conjectures, but truth, as the Jacksons know all too well, is a commodity as valuable as it is elusive.

Let us not forget that where there is dissent, there often lurks necessity. Dissent challenges us, forces us to confront uncom-fortable truths about ourselves and our values. It is the grit that produces the pearl, and yet, it is also a potential harbinger of chaos.

As Jacksons, we straddle the fine line between tradition and evolution, between maintaining the status quo and heeding the call for change. Our morals are the battlegrounds for our very identity. What do we value? Is it wealth, power, legacy? Or is it something more intangible, the unseen bonds that deter us, even as we stand?

The robes we wear tonight are heavier than usual, laden with the weight of decisions that will shape the lives of the Jacksons', the funghi and humans as well. In every thread, there is a story, in every fold, a secret. These robes, they know our true nature, our ambitions, our fears. They absorb our pride and our prejudice, becoming both our armour and our albatross.

The hour grows late, and the time for a decision draws near. Let us, therefore, proceed with the vote, bearing in mind that the true measure of our worth is not what we claim tonight, but what we hold dear in our hearts. May wisdom guide your hand, and may the bonds of blood hold, however tenuously, in the trials to come.

Now, as the gavel rests uneasily in my grasp, I recognize the gravity of the decisions that lie at our feet, decisions that venture into realms ethical, unthinkable, perhaps even abominable. It is with a wary mind that I lay before you the paths devised from the legal labyrinth of Marvin Jackson's will.

The first path is the initiation of what has been euphemistically termed the Human Harvesting Programme. This vision, proposed by our esteemed Marvin Jackson, calls for a venture into territories of intergalactic harvesting. Studies and studies have been laid out and the information we have obtained is available for every one of you. The ethical implications stagger the mind — the commodification of human essence, packaged neatly as a necessity for a higher level of consciousness to raise above. Yet, can we, should we, endorse such a course?

The second option before us is to maintain the status quo — to stand still, to let the currents of time and fate sweep us where they may. This path of inaction is, on its surface, the path of least resistance. It requires no decisions that might weigh heavily on our consciences in the years to come. However, consider this: to do nothing is a decision in itself, one that may lead us into stagnation or decline, as unresolved issues fester like wounds untended. Is our legacy to be one of indifference, characterized by a refusal to face the challenges that loom large on our horizon?

Lastly, we are presented with the option to prohibit outright all notions of human commodification. This would be a definitive stance, a clear declaration of our collective morality, asserting that some lines should never be crossed, no matter the potential gains in wealth or security. It is a choice that upholds the sanctity of human life and dignity above all else. But we must also ask ourselves — are we prepared to face the potential consequences, the sacrifices that such a prohibition entails?

As president of this committee, it is not my place to sway your judgment with personal biases. My role is to ensure that each voice is heard, that each vote is counted, and that the decision reflects not merely the will of one but the collective will of the Jackson lineage. Let us approach this plebiscite with the solemnity it deserves. Consider deeply, debate with both passion and compassion, and choose with the wisdom that this moment demands.

You will find before you three slips of paper, each representing one of the stark choices we face. Cast your vote secretly, let your conscience be your guide, and may we all have the courage to abide by the outcome, whatever it may be.

Remember, the future of the Jackson family, in all its moral and ethical dimensions, hangs in the balance. Tonight, under the weight of our forebears' gaze and the shadow of posterity's judgment, we define not just a legacy of wealth, but a legacy of values.

The time has come. Let us vote."

11

Editorial Reviews

Macarena Franceschini - https://www.linkedin.com/in/macarena-montes-franceschini/

Visiting fellow in Animal Law & Policy Program at Harvard Law School

"In *The Jackson's Debate*, Marqv Neves delivers a thought-provoking and humorous exploration of the ethics of eating animals. Set in an alien world, this short novel challenges human supremacy, forcing us to rethink our place in the world and leaving us feeling oddly alien to ourselves.

The premise is both simple and profound: a group of highly intelligent extraterrestrials debates whether humans should be harvested for consumption. On the one side are those who believe that, given the nutritional crisis impacting these aliens, consuming irrational, destructive creatures like humans would not violate their ethical principles if done correctly. On the other side, some take a more cautious approach, advocating for further studying human consciousness before making any decisions.

One of the book's most captivating aspects is the way aliens view nonhuman animals. Animals are considered sentient, rational beings capable of deep thought and communication. At one point, the aliens interview orcas, who offer their candid views about humans. The orcas describe us as chaotic, destructive, and lacking communication skills. This conversation provides a sharp critique of human behavior, framing us as a species that often misunderstands other animals, nature, and the things that truly matter.

This section is particularly timely, given recent scientific advances in communicating with cetaceans. Perhaps, in the near future, we will be able to ask whales and dolphins what they think of us. Will we listen if they tell us that the noise and speed from our vessels, our interference with their habitats, our fishing practices, oil extraction, and other practices cause distress to their communities? Will we stop these practices? Humans rarely pause to consider what other animals think of us. But we should, as this exercise could reveal the true scale of our destructive impact on animals and their communities.

As the aliens deliberate, the reader is subtly invited to adopt their perspective—to see the human species not as the center of the universe but as one species among many, perhaps not even the most rational or intelligent. The cleverness of Neves's writing lies in how it shifts the reader's point of view. By immersing us in the aliens' debate, the reader begins to feel alien themselves as though our human ways—our belief in superiority, our obsession with consumption, our pollution, and our disregard for other animals and nature—are no longer familiar but strange and absurd. We are confronted with our own assumptions about what it means to be human and what it means to *not* be human. It encourages readers to consider whether we truly are the rational, superior beings we imagine ourselves to be.

For anyone interested in the ethics of eating animals or in challenging the long-standing narrative of human supremacy, this book is a must-read. It's entertaining, accessible, and thought-provoking—perfect for anyone curious about their place in the world and how we relate to the animals with whom we share it. Fiction like this, along with the discussions it sparks, is a crucial way to challenge human supremacy, a belief so entrenched in society that literature, music, art, theater, and film are necessary tools to combat it and help us realize that we share the planet with many other sentient beings."

Vanessa Amoroso — https://www.linkedin.com/in/vanessaamoros o/

Head of Wild Animals in Trade, FOUR PAWS International; Vice Chair at Freedom for Animals

"Marqv Neves' The Jacksons' Debate is a thoughtful and provocative reflection on morality and interspecies ethics, told through the eyes of a highly advanced alien society grappling with an important question: should humans be seen as equals – or a resource? Not just for animal lovers and advocates, but for all, it's a story that shines a light on our own treatment of the creatures we share this world with.

The ethical discussions in the book mirror humanity's often uncomfortable debates about animal sentience and worth. The Jacksons' analysis of humans – their self-destructive habits and environmental harm – calls into question our own justifications for continuing to exploit animals. It's a sobering reminder of how easily power can obscure compassion.

What makes this story so poignant is the Jacksons' respect for life. Their thoughtful coexistence with their home's species highlights how humans, by contrast, often prioritize convenience over care. Their use of the Precautionary Principle – a commitment to act with caution when the impact is uncertain – is a beautiful and humbling example of ethical integrity.

This novella doesn't just challenge us; it invites us to reimagine what coexistence could look like if driven by understanding, empathy and kindness. It's a powerful, inspiring read for those passionate about animals and the Earth."

By Taylor Waters — https://www.linkedin.com/in/taylor-waters/

Doctor of Law (J.D.) at Michigan State University College of Law

A Thought-Provoking Look at Ethical Dilemmas: My Take on The Jacksons' Debate

As an animal lawyer and deontologist, The Jacksons' Debate by Marqv Neves left me both fascinated and unsettled. This speculative fiction flips the ethical script by putting humanity under the moral microscope of an alien species, forcing readers to confront uncomfortable truths about our treatment of non-human animals.

The premise—a society of advanced telepathic beings, the Jacksons, debating whether humans should be ethically consumed as food—is a provocative lens through which Neves critiques speciesism. The Jacksons' deliberations, particularly their attempt to define a "scale of sentience," hit close to home. It's eerily reminiscent of the arbitrary hierarchies we create to justify how we treat animals. As someone who works within legal frameworks meant to protect animals, I found myself reflecting on how often those frameworks are molded more by human convenience than by genuine respect for animal rights.

One aspect I found especially compelling was the character of Grag Jackson, who champions the Precautionary Principle. His call for restraint and further understanding of human sentience aligns with deontological ethics, where the duty to respect beings with intrinsic worth is paramount. The tension between Grag's caution and the more pragmatic (and morally dubious) arguments of his colleague Marvin serves as a brilliant parallel to real-world debates about how we justify exploiting animals for food, entertainment, or research.

The satirical elements of the book are sharp and effective. The Jacksons' bewilderment at human fashion trends, wastefulness, and contradictory behaviors often had me chuckling in recognition. Yet, that humor is undercut by the sobering realization of how these critiques mirror our larger societal failings, particularly in our relationship with the environment and other species.

For me, the book's greatest strength lies in its ability to evoke empathy through reversal. By positioning humans as the subject of moral debate, it forces us to confront how little voice we give to animals in decisions that shape their lives. It's a discomforting thought, but one that feels necessary.

If I had one critique, it's that the book sometimes leans so heavily into its thought experiment that the narrative can feel secondary. But perhaps that's the point. This isn't a story designed to comfort; it's meant to challenge and provoke, and it succeeds on those terms.

As someone deeply invested in both animal rights and ethical philosophy, I found The Jacksons' Debate to be a brilliant and unsettling reflection on the inconsistencies of human morality. It's a must-read for anyone willing to wrestle with the uncomfortable question: What would our actions look like under the scrutiny of a truly impartial gaze?

By Daniel Clark — https://www.linkedin.com/in/daniel-clark-wr iter/

Writer, Editor, Translator; Animal Rights Advocate; BA and MPhil from the University of Cambridge.

"This is not a novella in the traditional sense but a carefully constructed ethical mirror. By forcing us to view our own species from an alien perspective, marqv neves achieves a far-reaching critique of human supremacy. This is essay-as-story, where the narrative serves as a vehicle for profound philosophical engagement. The effect is familiar and deeply unsettling.

The Jacksons' Debate is a series of debates about eating another species. It is also an unflinching examination of the limits of human power. In his rigorous and riveting style, the author works through the ethical complexities involved in breeding, raising, slaughtering and eating non-human animals through an alien lens. In short, he passes under the microscope what is normally hidden from the consumer's sight.

Can our systematic treatment of other species ever be justified? Some Jacksons think so, as many humans do today. Yet neves asks us to look anew at the age-old debate. Stepping outside one's own biases can illuminate the strangeness in our everyday actions and beliefs. For example, the Jacksons' bewilderment at human clothing becomes a brilliant exploration of how we dismiss other species' behaviours as irrational simply because we fail to understand them.

Speculative fiction is an ideal genre through which to explore the ethical implications of eating animals. What the author eschews in narrative convention, he makes up for with his depth of ideas. That is not to say that the novella is aimed only at those with a philosophy degree; any reader who is prepared to engage with ethics, to sit with uncomfortable parallels and question long-held assumptions will be enriched by reading it.

Overall, *The Jacksons' Debate* succeeds not despite its philosophical bent but because of it. The novella represents a choice to use fiction as a medium for ethical debate. For readers willing to engage with its deeper questions, *The Jacksons' Debate* offers a mind-bending experiment in self-reflection."

Marina Rebelo—https://www.linkedin.com/in/your-ghostwriter/

Author Of Crystal Tear

"The Jackson's Debate is not just a simple novella but a profound philosophical narrative. By analysing the Human Race through the perspective of highly conscious aliens, Neves makes us question the absurdities and contradictions inherent in our daily lives. Whether it be our clothing habits or dietary choices, society seems to be playing a crucial role in how we live our lives and take care of our planet. This is pushing the reader to reconsider our ethics and the rational behind our actions. Each chapter has its own set of ethical questions, from sustainability to veganism or our fear of death.

Neves challenges us to scrutinise the reasons we provide for our treatment of other earthly species, questioning whether our perceived superiority is in natural order or simply a human made belief.

The aliens are very logic centric, and although their conscious is heightened, it makes us question what truly makes a sentient being. Is our consciousness the centre of our superiority or is it the society we created over the centuries, sculpting us into those irrational and non logical beings?

The philosophical aspect of the book confronts readers with uncomfortable truths and asks them to reassess their beliefs and practices. Rather than giving us full answers, Neves let us make our own decisions by opening up a debate on the human race and on what defines us as a species. This introspection leaves the reader with one question: Are we truly worthy of the planet we inhabit, or have we taken advantage of a presents from the universe (or a higher entity) without ever being grateful for this gift?

Less of a storytelling piece, more of a philosophy thesis, this book is a fantastic way to analyse what we have become as a species and what makes us worthy of living."

Dr Sabine Brels - https://www.linkedin.com/in/sabine-brels/

Director of World Animal Justice

"An extraordinary fusion of imagination and ethics, this ground-breaking fiction compels us to confront the silent injustices inflicted upon other species, inspiring a bold rethinking of humanity's role in creating a world of true compassion and justice for all living beings."

Micheall Hill - https://www.linkedin.com/in/michael-hill-52a8

881a7/

Lead Researcher at the THRIVE Project

Anthropocentrism and the way we view non-human animals are closely linked, with everything from extinction of species to biodiversity threats, to using animals for human purposes are linked to this. In this book 'The Jackson's Debate' the depiction of an alien species perceiving humans only as for their consumption illuminates the way that humans can at times perceive animal species, and showcases this issue through a fictional lens. The ethical considerations of one individual also highlights the concerns posed in the modern world, linked to anthropocentrism and how we as humans not only may cause the issue, but are capable of resolving it, through ethical deliberation, and recognising the incentives, both environmental and social for doing so.

At THRIVE Project we recognise the importance of this issue and through the use of the THRIVE Framework, and using the best science we showcase and illuminate paths forward for a thrivable future. Thrivability goes beyond mere sustainability, it is about not just break-even survival, it is about creating a prosperous and thrivable world for the future.

This issue as discussed within this book is important to be addressed, and is central to creating a Thrivable future! To learn more about the THRIVE Project, and the THRIVE Framework, visit our website, follow our webinar, podcast and blog series, you can also read our White Papers and Journal articles on the website.

https://thrivabilitymatters.org/about-thrive-project/

12

Acknowledgments

So, if you have come this far to the end of this book, it means you might be at least a little interested in how this project came to life—from the book itself to the "*Can Fiction Help Us Thrive*" initiative. *Can Fiction Help Us Thrive* is the beginning of a new branch of the THRIVE project, one that aims to spark reflection within the reader, but not in a direct, prescriptive way. Achieving a better world for all requires deep alterations in our ways of living and thinking, and to get there, every possible path for change in thought must be explored. THRIVE is about being innovative, about thinking outside the norm—so here we are, using fiction as a new way to spark that change.

A story is all about showing, not telling. When someone reads this novella, the experience they have—both rational and emotional—might lead them to see animal consumption differently. It could make them reconsider the real-world boundaries of sentience or provoke some other shift in perspective, even one that as the author, I may not have considered. That's the beauty of fiction: it offers a new lens, and it is up to the reader

115

to decide how they use it.

Bringing this unconventional idea to fruition was possible thanks to THRIVE's flexibility and openness toward its participants. At its core, THRIVE operates as a sociocracy—a concept I'll admit I wasn't familiar with before joining. But more importantly, it's not something you fully understand right away. There's no introductory meeting where everything is laid out for you—the goals, your role, how it all works. Instead, you learn as you go; the more you engage, the more you understand, and the more you benefit from being part of it. Every project THRIVE embraces comes from the willingness of its participants to make it happen. There may be moments when the enthusiasm is uneven, and it's up to those who believe in the vision to get others excited about it too.

In many ways, it reminds me of an ideal relationship—the glue that holds it all together is simply the willingness and belief of the people involved. There are no strict hierarchies, no obligations, no "holding accountable" in a traditional sense— only shared values and mutual trust.

To everyone who played a part in making this initiative possible, thank you. I hope this project prompts those who read it to reflect, to take steps in alignment with the shared goal of a better world for all living beings. And perhaps, in doing so, it might just create a better world for each individual as well.

With that said, I could not finish this story without recognising those closely in contact with me, who provide the platform for me to exist happily in the world, giving me the clarity and space to focus on creating this fictional story.

It starts with my parents, Daniele and Marcus Neves, and my sister, Carolina Neves—my cohort, my everyday companions. Our journey together has had its bumps, beginning with my arrival during their teenage years, growing up alongside them, and navigating shared goals and struggles. It was their unwavering drive and resilience that allowed us to thrive, making me a product of that chaotic environment—unconventional, perhaps, but filled with lessons in love, empathy, and an almost naive trust in the good intentions of those around me. Those qualities profoundly impacted me, influencing how I interact with the world and reflected in this book.

That sense of familial love and connection extends outwards, encompassing my wider family, who deserve as much thanks and recognition: my grandparents, Sonia and Jurandir Neves; my aunt, Simone Neves, and Mike Martins; my great uncles, Jorge da Silva and Reginal Ribeiro; and my cousins, Leonardo Neves, Luiza Neves, Fabio and Marcelle Palma, and their newest little ones, Mavie and Lutero.

Equal recognition belongs to my girlfriend, Isabella Fulton. I could never have foreseen the strength and depth of the relationship we've built. It has been an education in what it truly means to *live* together, to unravel and understand each other's ambitions, vulnerabilities, and insecurities–to carry them as if they were a part of my own experience. Learning to genuinely celebrate another person's joy and support their aspirations is a driver of growth and an unexpected gift.

I am certain our relationship is inextricably linked to the deep inner peace that has allowed me to explore this particular fictional theme, one so far removed from the objective nature of our lives. Spending so many hours caught up in this different reality, in the minds of fictional characters, was only possible because I knew that with Isabella, I was exactly where I wanted to be. I must also say that her support throughout this process, the insights from her reviews and comments, and her encouragement were all vital contributions that helped shape this final manuscript.

Finally, I must thank my friends and former work colleagues, Luisa Paiva and Caroline Freitas, who also happened to be important sounding boards during this project's development. They shared their thoughts on initial concepts, painstakingly read beta versions, and were tireless champions encouraging me to turn this idea into a reality. Sharing this creative process with them was incredible.

Afterword

As a law graduate and current Master's student in Sustainable Development at the University of Sussex, my main research topic revolves around human-animal relations, where I advocate for animal rights expansion. In this story, I aim to put this into perspective when an alien race philosophically discusses having humans as a food source. As I perceive it, most villains in the history of the world did not consider themselves to be villains, yet history has considered some to be and some not to be. Several paths have led us to cruelty and salvation; this story presents a quirky path that, understood as it is, may illuminate how oddly we might stumble into causing cruelty, even if considering ourselves ethical, advanced, sophisticated, and so on and so forth.

My aim with "The Jacksons Debate" is not to provide definitive answers to the ethical questions it raises, but rather to explore the complexities of those questions and the potential for bias even within a society that prides itself on being highly considerate and meticulous. The elongated philosophical debates are intentional, serving as a reflection of the Jacksons' personality and their tendency to engage in profound, sometimes rambling, discussions. The lack of a counterpoint perspective is also deliberate, highlighting the possibility of overlooking crucial aspects of reality, even when operating from a position of

119

perceived ethical superiority.

The story intentionally blends fiction with real scientific concepts to create a sense of plausibility and ground the narrative in a relatable context. This allows for a deeper exploration of the potential for constructing narratives that, while scientifically sound, may lead to morally questionable conclusions. The ultimate message is that scientific knowledge, while essential, does not necessarily dictate ethical imperatives.

About the Author

Marqv Neves is an advocate based in Rio de Janeiro, interested in exploring the ethical dimensions of coexistence. With a background in law and a master's in Sustainable Development from the University of Sussex, Marqv combines his legal expertise with his interest in fiction to challenge societal norms. He's also a researcher at the Thrive Project, where he contributes to building a future that recognizes and respects the rights of non-human beings.

You can connect with me on:

🌐 https://thrivabilitymatters.org

🐦 https://x.com/intent/post?text=Homepage&url=https://thrivabilitymatters.org

📘 https://www.facebook.com/thrivabilitymatters

🔗 https://www.linkedin.com/in/marcusnevesmarqv

Subscribe to my newsletter:

✉ https://thrivabilitymatters.org/newsletter

www.ingramcontent.com/pod-product-compliance
Ingram Content Group UK Ltd.
Pitfield, Milton Keynes, MK11 3LW, UK
UKHW021035050125
453207UK00009B/52

9 780646 707044